D1711603

BEARLY ACCIDENTAL

USA *TODAY* BESTSELLING AUTHOR

DAKOTA CASSIDY

Published 2017 by Dakota Cassidy.

ISBN: 978-1544729770

Manufactured in the USA.

Email dakota@dakotacassidy.com with questions or inquiries.

Bearly Accidental

Darling readers,

Thank you, thank you for your love and continued support of The Accidentals since I've gone indie. Their ongoing success is due in great part to all of you—and I can't ever thank you enough for helping me make this transition a painless one!

Author Note: *Bearly Accidental* is Book 12 in The Accidental Series and is connected to *Accidentally Ever After* (Book 11). If you don't wish to read spoilers, I recommend you read *Accidentally Ever After* first. Besides, *Ever After* has Nina in a yellow ball gown with big poofy hair and singing bluebirds circling her head. You don't want to miss that, do you?

Huge thanks to fellow author Fiona Jayde for her help with the Russian in this book. You're amazeballs!

Also: For anyone new to The Accidentals, I've included a link to *Interview With An Accidental*, a quick, totally free (and mostly painless) interview-style introduction to the women who are the heart and soul of this twelve-book series, originally published traditionally. If you're a repeat offender (YAY to repeat offending, you rebels!), skip right to chapter one!

Love,

Dakota XXOO

Dakota Cassidy | Bearly Accidental

Acknowledgements

Illustration: Katie Wood

Cover: Valerie Tibbs, Tibbs Design

Editor: Kelli Collins

Chapter 1

"I swear to God, ass-sniffer, if you don't slow the eff down, I'm gonna—"

A woman named Marty—or "ass-sniffer," as he'd heard—cut the pretty brunette off and, with hands on slender hips, bellowed into the cold late-afternoon air, "You're gonna what, Not-Mistress-Of-The-Dark-Anymore? Rip my intestines out via my throat and wrap them around the nearest tree? Tie them into a big girlie bow? Or wait—maybe you're gonna chew my face off? That's always high on your list of threats. But guess what, Dark One? You can't do that anymore, can you, Nina Statleon? Know why?"

Cormac Vitali winced. This Marty was taunting Nina. Outright daring her to take a shot at her. It was in her tone and in her stance. She'd been doing it since he'd discovered them here in the woods of Colorado while out on a run, and she hadn't let up since.

What made him wince was how the brunette would react. He didn't understand what the issue was between the two women, but the dark-haired woman was as testy as a sleeping bear poked with a stick.

Hah! Poking a bear. Funny, Cormac. You're a laugh riot these days.

Nina made a fist of her gloved hand in response, her teeth clenched tight in her streamlined jaw. She was as stunningly beautiful as she was disgruntled, with her scrunched-up face peeking out from the furred hood of her coat, her almond-shaped, coal-black eyes narrowed.

She jammed her hands inside the pockets of her thick black jacket, but her lips instantly stopped moving, save for puffing out condensation in harsh gasps as she fought her way up the snowy hill.

So the question was, why couldn't Nina chew Marty's face off anymore?

Obviously, this woman Marty knew why Nina couldn't chew her face off. Her question had certainly been asked rhetorically. Which made him curious, too. Who—on a regular basis, if Marty's words weren't an exaggeration—threatened to chew someone's face off? And why was this beautiful woman so damn violent?

Marty stopped in the middle of her seemingly effortless uphill climb through at least a foot of snow and winked over her shoulder with a saucy blue eye.

"What? No answer, Mouthy McMouth? S'okay. I got your answer riiight here, Snookie. You can't chew my face off or tie my intestines in a bow because you're—not—a—vampire anymore, Statleon! You have neither the strength nor agility to carry out said threat. So take a breather from the I'm-so-scary crap you're always flinging at everyone like a monkey with poop. In fact, just take a breather. You look positively winded."

Oh shit. This Nina wasn't just winded. She was winded and seething. And not a vampire anymore… Curious indeed.

Out of nowhere, the third woman of the trio appeared, moving into his line of vision from where he hid behind a thick pine tree.

She stomped across the length dividing the two women, kicking up packed snow like the ice was nothing more than a gaggle of dust bunnies, and held up a gloved hand with the speed and grace of a panther.

"For the love of all that's holy. Shut. *Up.* The both of you just shut your flappy lips! I'm sick to death of the bickering." The woman affected a hunched-at-the-shoulders posture with an angry expression, and growled, exactly like the brunette named Nina, "Aw, eff you, Miss Clairol 222. You don't know shit—zip your fucking piehole or I'll wax your damn eyebrows off!" Then she used a finger to twirl the length of her ponytail and bat her eyelashes as she said, in a breathy tone an octave higher, "I'd like to see you try, Faux Elvira! How will you ever catch me if you can't even get past the refrigerator without a pit stop for another batch of Buffalo wings?"

Both the blonde Marty and the brunette Nina openly gaped at this woman—tall, elegant, and one helluva referee—as though *she* were the one who'd gone mad.

Now she waggled her finger, swishing it at the women. "Don't you two look at me all wide-eyed and aghast while you clutch your proverbial pearls like you haven't the faintest idea what I'm talking about. *Don't even.* Since Nina's vampiric demise in Shamalot, if she's not stuffing her gullet with food, she's arguing with *you*, Marty. Who, I might add, just can't seem to let it go. Okay, so Nina has no powers anymore and she doesn't want them back. She's reveling in her returned humanity. So the hell what? If she had no legs, would you razz her like this?"

Marty pursed her lips in thought, her soft cheeks sporting two bright red spots. "Could we try the scenario where she has no mouth as our example for today, Principal Wanda?"

"Shut it! Shut it now, or I swear on your fruity color wheels I'll GD well kill you, Blondie!" Nina bellowed, her husky voice reverberating around the forest as she attempted a run at Marty, only to get caught up in her bulky boots.

"Again I ask, how?" Marty yelped back with devilish glee. "A chicken wing to my head, perhaps? A six-pack of brewskies to the throat? A slip and fall in a melted puddle of the gallons of ice cream you've consumed since Shamalot?"

Wanda the Elegant lost it then. Something Cormac rather had the notion she didn't do often. In fact, the entire time he'd been tracking them, she'd not been the least ruffled as they'd charged through the snow, battled a squall of even more of the white stuff (bickering the entire way), and eventually landed mere moments from the cabin he'd so carefully pieced back together away from prying eyes.

But right now, Wanda's eyes grew all hot and furious, while her spine went rigid. "*Eeeenough!*"

Aw hell. She'd yelled so loudly, snow from the branches of the tree he was beneath shed in icy clumps, thumping to the ground and just missing his head.

Obviously, Wanda had been dealing with the sort of grief these two doled out on a fairly regular basis, and her eyeballs were floating from trying to keep her head above water.

"I won't have this anymore—understand?" she said with a hiss. "We're here for Toni, got it? All the rest of the crazy from Shamalot, like Nina losing her powers and making cheesecake the new breakfast, will have to wait. Got it? We have a lead, ladies, a solid lead after a month-long search for Cormac. Are we going to do what we came to do for Toni or are we going to continue this pointless argument about Nina's choice not to return to her vampiric ways? Because honestly, I'm up to my eyeballs. It's not up to *you* to help Nina find a way to become undead again, Marty. Nina didn't have a choice when she became a vampire. It was an accident. She can certainly choose not to be one now. It doesn't mean she's less our friend if she remains human. We just have to adjust to her human needs."

Wait. What the what? Toni was alive? They knew his sister Antonia? They knew *him*? And where the hell was Shamalot?

Cormac wasn't sure whether he should bust out from behind the tree and demand they explain why they were looking for him and how they knew Toni, or if he should continue to eavesdrop before making a final judgment call.

Marty bristled, adjusting her blue knit hat. "You mean like adjust to the fact that she's slower than molasses uphill in the winter time—literally—or that she's always whiny and cold now? Or that she's no longer the muscle of this trio yet continues to behave like Thug Lite? Fine. Forget it all. She can do whatever she wants to do. I agree. Don't be undead, for all I care. But quit your bitching about not being able to keep up with us to a minimum while you fill your big mouth with whatever isn't nailed down, or I just might see if intestines really *can* be yanked out by way of your ever-increasing gut!"

Ohhh, Marty sure was damn angry Nina had chosen humanity. Almost as though being human was going against her belief system—a betrayal of some kind. But wait. Were Marty and Wanda vampires, too?

How could *he* tell? He was still learning to parse scents, but he had no clue what a vampire would smell like anyway.

Nina's deep dark eyes went wide with hot fury, her next question asked in total girlish horror. *"Did you just call me fat?"*

Marty sucked her cheeks in, making her lips purse, as though she were utterly appalled. "I did no such thing. I said *a* body part was increasing. Which, like I've been saying, isn't a surprise, seeing as you've made it your mission to work your way through an entire ice cream case at the grocery store one pint of Ben & Jerry's at a time."

Nina pulled one of her hands from her incredibly bulky down jacket and gave Marty the finger before she began an awkward attempt to unwrap a bite-size Snickers with gloves so thick, she fumbled and dropped it smack in the snow.

"Oh, fuck you, Werewolf. If you couldn't eat real food for eight GD years like the blood diet I've been on, once you got your hands on some vittles, your ass'd be the size of a freightliner. Wait. It *is* the size of a freightliner. So quit paranormal-shaming and piss the hell off!"

Picking up the fallen Snickers, Nina held it up to the sky, kissed it and popped it in her mouth, smiling in defiance at Marty as she chewed.

Okay, so Marty was a werewolf. Arooooooo.

Interesting.

Wanda closed her eyes before lifting her face to the heavens and blowing out a disgusted sigh.

Clearly, she'd asked the universe for patience on more than one occasion.

When her eyes popped open again, she looked as though she'd come to terms with her lot in their friendship. "Look, if the two of you are going to argue, I'll just do this alone. We're here to find Cormac, and find Cormac I darn well will. After what the Great and Wonderful Roz told us, we need to find him. All we have to do is locate him, fix the problem, and we go home. Now, I'm going to do that. With or without you two pains in my derriere."

With that, Wanda stomped up the hill at a speed so rapid; he almost couldn't believe he was actually witnessing a feat so incredible.

But then he reminded himself, *you turn into a grizzly bear at random, moron.* At least, that's the breed of bear he thought he was, but it was all still very unclear. Even after three years and fifty or so romance novels on the subject of bear shifting—his only resource for research.

And hello. What was there to find at all unusual about a woman who moves at the speed of light or, for that matter, a werewolf and a former vampire who knew someone named the Great and Wonderful Roz?

Nothing. That's what. Who was he to discriminate when all he needed was a mama bear and baby bear to complete this nightmare of a fairytale gone painfully awry?

So whoever these women were, they were like him—whatever that meant. They clearly understood what had happened to him. And they knew his sister.

And she is alive.

Christ, Cormac had to hold on to the tree he was propped up against to keep from crashing to the floor of the forest in relief.

All this time, three solid years, hiding out in this prison that was frozen more often than not, trying to find out what happened to Toni without being discovered himself had been a continual nightmare.

So why not go and introduce yourself to the nice, if not squabbly ladies, Cormac? Find out what they're up to?

Because how did they know Toni? Maybe they worked for Stas, the fuck who'd kidnapped his sister to begin with and owned every cop this side of the universe. Maybe these women were just his polite henchmen. Okay, so the Nina woman wasn't so nice, but maybe these paranormal people stuck together, and finding Cormac meant they got some kind of bounty.

He did have very sensitive information—even if the police wouldn't take him seriously.

You're paranoid—she is alive and well, Vitali. Look at them—look at all three of them. All drama doused with perfume, pricey boots, and potty mouths. Do they really look capable of working for a freak like Stas?

No. But one could never be too paranoid when it came to what had happened to him and Toni three years ago. Nope. He was going to silently wait this one out.

The last time he'd rushed, he was turned into a goddamn grizzly bear.

So wait he damn well would.

Quietly. From behind them, as they all began to move upward and far too close to his cabin for comfort.

Flexing his fingers, he felt the phantom ache of his missing digit, hacked off by none other than Stas himself, a total maniac who just happened to be his sister Toni's ex-boyfriend and a mid-level player in a much bigger Russian mob organization.

A noise behind him, subtle, maybe even only in his mind, made him forget about the ache in his finger and stand up straight.

Cormac tilted his head again and sniffed the air. If there was anything valuable in this crazy-ass transformation he'd gone through, it was his heightened sense of smell.

It was badass. He could scent a fish from a mile down the creek, a bush full of ripe berries football fields away. In fact, in the beginning of whatever had happened to him, he could scent everything. For a time, it had been unnerving, but over the course of the last three years, he'd grown accustomed to it, nurtured it, and read fiction to try to understand it.

And what he smelled was perfume. Light, fruity. Maybe peaches and tangerines? None of the three women were wearing anything fruity. In fact, Nina wasn't wearing anything at all but the scent of Buffalo wings and Coors Light with a hint of Kit Kat bar.

Cormac whipped around as the women continued upward, closer and closer to the only place he felt even remotely safe.

His eyes scanned the dollops of snow like whipped cream on the trees, the landscape hilly and covered in rocks, looking for this new scent, but seeing nothing.

Must be his damned imagination.

"Wait the fuck up, for Christ's sake!" Nina yelled to her counterparts, struggling to push her way through the deep snow. "Jesus, this isn't the flippin' Olympics, Color Wheel Queen!"

"I told you that backpack would weigh you down, didn't I? You only have a side of beef in it. Now pick up the pace, Ex-Vampire!" Marty shouted back, her devilish giggle swirling around the forest like tinkling fairies.

"I was packing just in case, all right? You don't know how the fuck long we're gonna be out here in the Hundred Acre Wood. I wanted to be prepared," she gasped.

"Hah! You could feed a small country with what's in that backpack and it has nothing to do with anyone but you and your bottomless pit of a stomach!" Marty chirped."

"One more crack about my fat keister and I'll haul your ass up that mountain and drop you from the tippy-top!"

As Cormac listened to them argue, following behind them, hopping from tree to tree, snowdrift to snowdrift, he caught the scent again, distracting him from formulating a plan about what to do with these women.

Sweet and soft, it grazed his nostrils before it slipped away.

He'd purposely covered his scent the moment he'd spotted the three of them from across the river. It seemed ridiculously cautionary at the time, but he'd learned the hard way never to expose himself. Now that he knew at least one of them was a werewolf, he was glad he'd taken the time to roll in some mud and leftover fish guts.

Just as the women peaked the top of the hill and Wanda yelled out, "Oh my God, I think I found it!" he smelled that perfume again.

That was probably five seconds before something sharp and pointy jabbed him in the side of his neck and he howled his outrage, before falling to the frozen ground and passing out cold.

Chapter 2

As the great Sheldon would say, bazinga!

Theodora "Teddy" Gribanov smiled in satisfaction as she eyed her prey from more than a hundred yards away.

Hah. Her older twin brothers, Vadim and Viktor, could essentially suck it. She still had it and she had it hard. Grabbing her phone from her backpack, she zoomed in and snapped a picture of Cormac Vitali's still body, lying in the snow as though he were merely napping, and sent it off to her brother with the subject, "Neener-Neener-Neener!"

Jamming the phone back into her pack, she hauled it over her shoulder and pushed her way up the small incline to stand over this enormous man she'd just taken down with a dart gun.

He was worth a lot of money.

A lot. Money she'd gladly collect and stuff away in her bank account until the time came to figure out how to save the part of her life that was her heart and soul.

For right now, all she wanted to do was teach her mouthy brothers a lesson about patience and perseverance, and the fact that, despite their ribbing her about being a candy-ass, she wasn't such a rainbow Skittle after all.

For a moment, she wondered who those women Cormac had been following were and if they were here for the same reason she was.

That would piss her off. A deal was a deal, *comrade*. Vitali was hers—which meant she needed to move quickly in case they'd heard his yelp through all that squealing they were doing up over the rise of the hill.

Kneeling, she was relieved to hear the voices of the three bickering women were still distant, but she couldn't quite catch what they were saying.

Not that it mattered. She was going to haul Cormac Vitali out of this forest, lob him into her battered truck and bring him in—then do a drive-by at the bank, where she'd withdraw her hefty paycheck.

Jamming her hands under his torso, she ignored how muscly he was, how thick his thighs were, and the fact that he had silky chestnut-brown hair sprouting from beneath his knit cap.

She also managed to ignore his stench. Why he'd covered himself in mud, fish guts, and whatever that salty hint of schmeg was, she had no clue.

Don't worry about who he is or what his predicament is, Teddy. It's what makes you too soft for this shit. Toughen up and imagine dollar signs on his forehead instead of trying to peer into his soul to see if his heart beats true. Bad guys are bad guys.

Viktor's taunting but stern words just before she'd left Denver came back to haunt her.

Okay, so she liked to look further than the paycheck. But looking at Cormac, his eyelashes fluttering against his ruddy cheeks, lean and chiseled, wasn't hard to do.

If one of her brothers had just tranq'd a hot babe, she'd entirely expect them to wonder what had brought their prey the misfortune of meeting the stealthy tip of a dart gun.

But they were slobbering Neanderthals, and they cared about one thing and one thing alone. Cash.

Well, to be fair, they cared about her, too. Which was why they'd taken her out of the game for so long.

But she was better now.

You're nothing, Teddy. Nothing.

Fuck you, she silently spat.

Teddy bit the inside of her cheek to fight the nausea. She damn well *was* better, and it was time to stop being the biggest sissy this side of the Mountain time zone and get 'er done. She needed this money.

Her hands only shook a little as she pulled Cormac's limp form to her chest, and she was proud to say she flung his body over her shoulder fireman style, her knees only buckling a little before she wobbled and righted herself, her teeth tightly clamped.

Rolling her head from side to side to ease the tension in her neck, she grunted as she began to make her way down the hill.

Jesus, he was heavy, and the fact that he was out cold made him heavier. Condensation puffed from her lips as she dragged her still-out-of-shape body down the hill and toward the river. She'd better pump up her jam if she hoped to get him to the truck and tie him down before the effects of the dart gun wore off.

But then two things happened at once.

Those three loud, constantly arguing women must have caught sight of her because there was a whole lot of caterwauling coming at her from behind.

Simultaneously, Cormac stirred, struggling against the hold she had on him at the back of his knees.

"What the fu…?" he yelped. His upper body, thick against her smaller shoulder, began to rear up.

She'd had a bad feeling the tranq gun didn't have enough sedative in it to contain someone his size, but she'd doubted her assessment at the last minute and decided to only nail him with one dart.

Just another poor judgment call on her part, she thought with a grunt as Cormac wrapped his arms around her thighs and, with his abs of steel, managed to take her down by tipping her backward, using the weight of his body and the press of his bent knees. They fell against the packed snow, making her cry out on impact and sending her backpack flying.

He rolled from her and, before Teddy even realized where he was, Cormac pounced, pushing her back into the snow, knocking the wind right out of her.

"For the love of fuck, what's going on, Marty?" one of the women bellowed as she ran down the hill, just as the other two appeared above Teddy.

Two lovely, put-together women with eyes of ragey-ish suspicion and their hands on their slender hips.

"Oh! Aren't you pretty? Doesn't she have lovely eyes poking out from that ugly-ugly mud-brown hat, Wanda?" the blonde with sparkling sapphire-blue eyes asked.

"Not the time for a color wheel assessment, Marty!" said the woman with an air of sophistication and the smoothest hair she'd ever seen in all of Colorado.

Teddy attempted to shake the snow from her face and wrestle her way out from beneath this enormous beast of a man. She was no weakling, but damn he was strong.

Gripping her wrists with a single calloused hand, Cormac yanked them over her head, pulled the dart from his neck and hurled it to the ground, then growled down at her, full of fire and brimstone, "*Who* the hell are you?"

The woman who's going to slap your ass in the pokey and collect a lot of cash? Probably not the way introductions should go if she was to keep her identity a secret.

Teddy attempted to struggle in his GI Joe grip of kung-fu steel one more time—and that was when she caught sight of his eyes.

They were green. Okay, so yeah, they were angry, too, but she saw beyond that.

Oh, sweet-sweet mother of pearl, his eyes were so green. Beautiful orbs in his head that shone like colored glass. Sharply defined jaw and cheekbones, ruddy skin and a beard of thick, coarse-looking hair on his face, all giving him that hot, casually laid-back look.

Teddy's heart sped up again as he settled on her torso completely—and a tingle of heat in her belly swished upward to her cheeks as she got an even closer look.

Thick lashes gave the appearance of guy-liner, but in her gut, she knew a man like Cormac would never wear makeup. He was too gruff—too involved in other things to care about his appearance enough to be concerned about how to enhance that thick fringe of lashes and make his eyes stand out.

Teddy's breath left her chest in a whoosh of air as he straddled her with thick thighs and his eyes bore a hole in her face.

But his anger didn't matter. None of that mattered. What mattered was what she had just discovered.

Jesus Christ, how could this be?

"*Who are you?*" He ground out the demand.

"I—"

"Cormac!" the pretty blonde—Marty—shouted, yanking at his shoulder. "You're hurting her! Get off!"

Who was this woman and why did she care if he was hurting her? Did they know each other? As she'd tracked Cormac tracking them, that wasn't the impression she'd had at all.

His head swiveled upward, his eyes blazing hot. "For that matter, who the hell are *you* two?"

"Three!" the gorgeous brunette, Nina—wrapped up like she was planning a move to Antarctica—wheezed out as she stumbled down the hill, stopping short next to Marty and placing her hands on her knees in order to catch her breath. "Holy shitballs, it's Lumberjack Bob."

"Who are you people and what the hell do you want with me?" Cormac looked back down at Teddy, his eyes glowing with suspicion and rage. "Are you with them, too?"

Teddy only managed to shake her head, still in utter disbelief. This was wrong. Everything was all wrong!

Wanda, the one who'd managed to keep the other two from ripping each other's throats out, gripped Cormac's shoulder, huffed out a breath, and gave him a good hard shove, sending him tumbling off Teddy and into the snow with his grunt lingering in the air.

"Marty said get off! Now, do not move a muscle until we're able to explain ourselves," she ordered from tight lips with a wave of her finger, her chest puffing up and down. "Or so help me, I'll take you out myself! I've had enough of everyone ignoring my wishes. Now hear this! I've had it up to my cerebellum with playing peacemaker for four days since we began this journey. You, Cormac Vitali, have the unfortunate circumstance of being my last damn straw. And don't doubt for a single second I can't take out a big, burly boy like you either. I'll knock you clear to Kentucky. So you march your muscled ass on up that hill to your cabin, you do it without complaint, and you do it *now*, or so help me, as Charles Manson is my witness, I'll kill you all! *Goooo!*"

Teddy's eyes followed the direction of Wanda's finger. This woman, whoever she was, had clearly had enough.

That was when she jabbed her finger down at Teddy, her eyes narrowed, her nostrils flaring. "That means you, too! I don't know who you are or what you want, but we're going to find out. And I'll take the dart gun, Annie Oakley, thank you very much!" She reached for the backpack and threw it over her shoulder.

Teddy began to protest, but Wanda clamped her fingers together right under her nose. "I said *not a word*. Not a single word, or you'll be the first on my list of things to kill while in Colorado. Got it? Get up and wallllk, goddamn it!"

Teddy only briefly looked into Wanda's pretty blue eyes, acknowledging she had an air of authority that couldn't be denied, before she crab-walked on her hands to back away from her. Rather than thicken the pot with confrontation, she hopped to her feet and began walking.

Marty followed Teddy closely while Nina, who looked absolutely frozen, fell in behind them.

There was nothing but silence as they made their way to the top of the hill and Cormac's cabin came into view.

The entire time, Teddy attempted to construct a story in her head to explain why she was in the middle of nowhere, hauling Cormac away like she was some sort of female variation on a Neanderthal—because Wanda would want a story. Oh yes, she would. She didn't look like the kind of woman who would put up with any shit.

When Teddy finally caught sight of Cormac's cabin, she wondered how he'd found this place. She'd never, in all her tracking, encountered this section of the forest, and she knew the forest like the back of her hand.

It was a crude structure under the purple and orange twilight of the coming evening. The logs sturdy, but with no particular architecturally appealing design to them. There was a lone folding chair by the front door, sandwiched between two bushes and an enormous pine tree. Maybe a fishing cabin?

Smoke wisped upward out of the brick chimney, and a sagging clothesline off to the right side of the cabin, with a metal bucket beneath, waved in the light wind.

More snow began to fall, the distant roar of a rushing creek filling her ears. God, it was beautiful here. Even under these daunting circumstances, Teddy had to admit, she loved the forest far more than she loved the lights of the city.

What she probably *wasn't* going to love? Explaining herself.

Cormac stopped at his front door, painted—of all things—an odd shade of eggplant purple, and turned to face them as they gathered, waiting for him to admit them entry.

"Well, open the door, dude. Jesus, it's like frickin' Iceland out here," Nina demanded with a shiver, her lips dry and cracked.

But Teddy didn't pay as much attention to Nina's grousing as she did the smells these women gave off, assaulting her nose, one right after the other. Foreign, tangy, one even brought to mind the word "displaced," if you could in fact smell such a thing. But it was strong.

She hadn't heard all of their conversations in detail. Most of it had been just bits and pieces. She'd heard their names, seen their arms waving and middle fingers flying, sensed some general discontent, but she'd been so focused on capturing Cormac, she'd clearly missed something important.

As Cormac looked down at them, his gaze piercing, Teddy refocused her thoughts and waited. "I don't know what's going on, but this is as far as it goes until you explain who you are and what the hell you want from me."

Then he crossed his arms over his burly chest to further the notion he wasn't budging.

But it didn't look like these women were up for any arguments. Especially the elegant one who'd demanded Teddy come with them to the cabin.

Wanda, the lady who'd shouted the orders, pushed her way past everyone and poked a finger into Cormac's wide chest. "Open the door or I'll use you as my battering ram. Got me, Bruiser? It's been a long damn afternoon. We've been out on this hike from Hades for four bloody days. I'm cold. I'm tired. I'm done with every single person around me complaining about everything—and I do mean *everything*. Now, I get your suspicion, but you're just going to have to trust that we're the good guys, or I'm going to steamroll right over you if you so much as squeak a peep from your gorgeous lips."

"But—"

Wanda clearly, visibly, undeniably snapped then. Her eyes went wild and furious, her mouth formed a sneer, and without so much as a grunt of exertion, she did exactly as promised. She steamrolled him, knocking Cormac, who was easily six-three and a good two-twenty, flat on his back.

Then, as dainty and graceful as any prima ballerina and just shy of pirouetting over his body, she hopped over him and entered the cabin, brushing the snow from her ski pants.

Cormac groaned from the ground, running a hand over his head, but the brunette held out her hand to him with a cackle. "Need some help, big boy? C'mon. Get up before Wanda whips out her clangers and things get really serious." Then she cackled again as Marty grabbed Teddy by the hand and dragged her into the cabin behind her.

Once inside, when she got a good look at the interior of the cabin, Teddy's mouth fell open on a gasp that took even her by surprise.

It was like FBI command central—or some special-ops mission.

Shit. What had her brothers gotten her into? Was this some kind of military facility—an outpost, maybe? Computer after computer lined the back wall, leaving only space for the hearth of the fireplace to the right, where a roaring fire burned, a small couch with mismatched cushions sitting in front of it.

There were monitors with all sorts of mugshots of some pretty rough-looking men, and maps with all manner of scrolling feeds of some kind.

But it didn't look terribly official. Not from the way it seemed he'd jerry-rigged a bunch of tech she didn't understand and several modems.

Wouldn't it just figure this guy was of the tinfoil hat variety? Maybe some kind of doomsday prepper? It made sense, living all the way out here in the woods as far as he could get from civilization. He was probably one of those conspiracy theory nuts with a YouTube channel and more guns than the Armed Forces combined.

Wanda, who'd knocked Cormac down as if he were made of nothing more than tissue paper, ground out another order. "Sit. *All of you*. Anywhere. Introductions are in order." She dragged her gloves from long, slender fingers and laid them over the crook in her arm before she folded them over her chest.

When everyone hesitated, she sneered and bellowed, "Do it!"

Teddy dropped where she was, crossing her legs and pulling her hiking boots up under her, right along with everyone else—except for Cormac, who had the audacity to resist.

Somebody was gonna lose their balls...

Because Wanda wasn't havin' it. She sauntered toward him, her eyes ablaze, her cheeks sucked inward. "You want another piece of this?" she taunted in a comical Brooklyn accent, pounding her chest with her palms.

As though he realized he'd be foolish to defy her for even one more moment, Cormac actually blanched and dropped down next to Teddy, but it wasn't without an expression of palpable silent protest. He oozed defiance from every pore of his sexy-sexy brickhouse body.

"Thank you. So, how about we go around the room and introduce ourselves? I'm Wanda Schwartz-Jefferson from Staten Island, New York. Married, wrangler of the WrestleMania Twins, occasional dabbler in the authorial pool."

Everyone remained silent until she nudged Marty with her toe.

"Oh! I'm Marty Flaherty from Buffalo, New York. Cosmetics company owner, mother, businesswoman, fashionista. Pleasure to meet you all."

Wanda glared at Teddy, making her face flush hot and red. "Oh, sorry. Um, Theodora...uh...Jackson—Denver, Colorado. Wildlife rescuer, single, helluva Sudoku solver." She cleared her throat, looking down at the floor and its colorful braided rugs. It wasn't exactly a lie.

She was a crappy liar so she'd kept it brief, but no way was she telling them what she was really doing here. Nuh-uh.

Wanda's gaze turned to the brunette, who was busily fishing through her backpack. She pulled out a Ziploc bag with a squashed sandwich in it and held it up like it was the biggest catch of the day. "Thank fuck. Found it!"

Marty rolled her eyes and unzipped her sky-blue down vest, shrugging it off to reveal a sapphire-blue turtleneck and colorful paisley scarf. "Phew. I was so worried you'd starve to death, you human garbage can."

Wanda hissed in Marty's direction before tapping Nina the Discontent on the shoulder. "Before you shove that in your mouth, use your words and introduce yourself."

The brunette sighed, expelling a raspy breath. "What is this, fucking *Romper Room*? Nobody gives a shit who we are as people. I don't give a shit who *they* are either. We don't need a round-robin of bullshit surface stuff to do what we gotta do."

Wanda swiped the sandwich bag from her friend's hand, held it up for a brief moment, a maniacal gleam in her eye, then dropped it to the ground and stomped on it, flattening it until the plastic broke and what looked like tuna oozed out from the crust.

Everyone gasped. Even Cormac.

"*I said*, introduce yourself."

Nina made a face up at Wanda but then she peeled off her thick black gloves and said, "Nina Statleon. Hungry. Cold. Hate everyone."

Marty clapped her hands, a set of bangle bracelets clinking together. "Yay! Look at you, using your words and emotions."

Nina scraped the crushed sandwich bag off the floor after she flipped Marty the bird.

When it was Cormac's turn, Teddy turned to look at him, the lines of his face chiseled in granite, a tic in his unmoving jaw. Talk about a long simmer—he was like a Crock-Pot of slow burn.

Nina, who sat on the other side of him, elbowed him in the ribs. "C'mon, dude. I don't want to see you lose your sacs in front of everybody. Plus, I wanna get the fuck out of here pronto. I like the woods as much as any bitch, but this shit for four days solid is for the birds. All this Grizzly Adams trees and fucking caribou just ain't my rap, yanno? So stop prolonging my agony and play the game so I can get on up outta here. If you do, I'll share my Combos with you. I got a shitload of 'em," she coaxed with an enticing shake of her backpack and a grin that decidedly mocked.

When Cormac finally spoke, he sent a chill up along Teddy's spine. Calm, his voice was like silk washed in honey. Rich and deep with a hint of a rasp.

"You already know who I am. The question is, why are you here and *how* do you know who I am?"

Wanda let out a sigh, crossing her feet at her furry-booted ankles. "We're here to help you, Cormac. Toni sent us."

Instantly, Teddy was on alert, coiled and ready to spring. *Who* was Toni?

Cormac cracked his knuckles, making a sucking noise with his teeth as though he was preparing for confrontation and his restraint was close to coming undone. "How do you know Toni?"

It was then that Wanda must have realized Teddy had no relation to this scenario—whatever this scenario was—and from the masked expression taking over her face, Teddy guessed Toni was private.

Which was the moment Wanda set her sights on Teddy, and she realized she needed an alibi. Fast.

Wanda's perfectly plucked eyebrow rose. "Why exactly are you here, Theodora?"

Yeah, Theodora, what brings you to the outermost reaches of the Colorado forests, with a dart gun, no less? Hmmmm?

Better stall.

"Teddy, please. You can call me Teddy," she said, hoping her voice wouldn't crack while she hatched a story in her busy brain.

Wanda swung her long arms in front of her and latched her fingers together in a basket. "Okay, *Teddy*," she drawled, her tone making Theodora squirm. "What brings you to Cormac's—with a dart gun?"

"It's kind of hard to explain…"

"Aw, fuck," Nina spat with disgust. "Here we go. Listen, Kitten Pants, spit it the shit out. Just do it and get it over with because if you don't, I'll miss dinner with my kid for the fourth night in a row since we got to this strange land of fucking icicles and free-range moose."

Wanda reached down and tugged on a long length of Nina's incredibly shiny, unbelievably thick almost-black hair. "Shut up." Then she turned that I-have-ways-of-making-you-talk gaze back to Teddy. "How about you try? And I suggest you try really hard or this could turn into an incredibly long night of epic, unpleasant proportions for you."

Nina cackled that cackle that said she took pleasure in another's pain. "Oh, hold the hell up now. If we're talkin' Wanda and torture, don't say a word, lady. I'd be willing to give up one more night of missed grub if she's gonna put the screws to you."

Marty reached around Nina and gripped the cap of her shoulder, making Nina wince and shrink back until there was the glisten of a tear in her eye.

"Get off, ass-sniffer! That stings!" Nina growled.

But Teddy held her hands up as white flags. "Okay. I'll try to explain. I'm here because…"

Because O-M-G, what, Teddy? What-what-whaaaat?

Wanda sucked in her cheeks, turning her peachy-glossed lips into that of a fish. Meaning she was gonna lose her shit if Teddy didn't answer.

She swallowed hard before she blurted out, "Because Cormac is my life mate!"

Chapter 3

You've done it now. You might as well have told him you planned your wedding on Pinterest and picked out names for your forthcoming children, Teds. Jesus, girl.

Teddy winced as silence pervaded the room. Silence and shock. Mouths fell open, eyes widened, and there was a snort from the appointed queen of snark.

That had come out all wrong. Way faster than she'd planned. She'd wanted to do a bit of warm-up to the subject. Maybe explain where she came from, and a bit about her background, her family, before making such an outlandish statement; hopefully get Wanda of The Schoolmarm Gaze of Death off her back.

But no, much like everything else in her life, relationships, bungee jumping, hotdog-eating contests, she'd hurtled headlong into the fire.

"Have you spent too much time watching *Lifetime* movies and tending your brood of cats?" Cormac asked in disbelief, leaning away from Teddy as though she'd just told him she was from the planet Pluto.

Which might be easier to process at this point.

Teddy shook her head and inhaled, feeling a headache forming right between her eyes. "No. Please, let me explain."

Nina dragged a bag of cheese popcorn from her backpack and ripped it open, stuffing a handful in her mouth. "Yeah. Explain, Theodora."

She smiled at Teddy. Beautiful, damn near perfect in fact, and maniacal, as though she enjoyed the most awkward of situations.

"So is it your habit to shoot all your life mates with dart guns and carry them out of the forest like sacks of potatoes? Some kind of ritualistic hunt for anything with a penis I missed the memo on?" Wanda asked, suspicion written all over her classically gorgeous features.

Teddy frowned and winced. "No. That was…it was an accident. I was just…just practicing while I…"

"So you could get it right when the time came to knock out your unwitting, very unwilling life mate?" Cormac asked, disbelief still heavy in his tone.

She paused at the way in which he used the words life mate. He didn't sound surprised by the term, only that she'd claimed he was hers.

"No! Look, I'm sorry. I was target practicing, I still had some darts in my backpack. I just didn't realize they were tranquilizer darts."

Liar, liar, pants on so much fire!

Nina popped her lips while pushing her way out of the heavy parka she wore, kernels of cheese popcorn falling to her crossed legs. "Ya know, I gotta give it to her. That's a pretty good line of bullshit. Very creative. Two thumbs up."

Teddy licked her dry lips, digging herself in deeper. "I work at a wildlife preservation called Sanctuary, in Denver. You can look it up on your vast array of computers if you'd like. Sometimes we have to tranquilize an injured animal and it's important to get it right the first time you take a shot. I was just killing time while I looked for Cormac…I'm sorry."

Ugh.

Marty's brow furrowed. "But you said you were here because Cormac is your um, life something or other, right? What does that mean?"

Ah. Now Teddy had the upper hand. Marty was a crappy liar. She damn well knew what a life mate was because she came from a circle of people who thrived on them. However, they didn't know she knew.

And Teddy knew they were all paranormal, from all the fighting they did as she'd tracked them. She just didn't know exactly what kind of paranormal. The word vampire had been used, but she didn't know how to identify scents of paranormal species other than that of her own kind.

One thing she definitely knew? The reason Cormac had covered his scent—because he was a bear.

Just like her.

Rather than stay on the floor where she felt small and overpowered, a feeling she didn't relish, Teddy rose with caution, keeping her palms facing outward.

"Okay, so let's just be honest here. It means that I know you're all paranormal—and Nina was once paranormal."

"Ohhh!" Nina squealed her delight, pounding her fist on her backpack. "Boom, baby! Shit just got real!"

Wow, this woman really did take extreme pleasure in the awkward.

Wanda's eyes flashed angry and bright as she approached. "And you know this how, *Teddy?*"

Teddy folded her hands in front of her and edged backward. Wanda's wrath was real, and she didn't want to invoke any more than was necessary.

"I don't mean to be disrespectful, but you guys were really loud out there in the forest. So, I sort of heard bits of your conversations about vampires and all. But I'm still not sure *what* you are."

Marty rasped a sigh and shook her head in obvious understanding. She swiped her index finger in the air. "That's what that smell is. It's you!" She pointed at Teddy. "I don't mean to offend. I mean, I honestly thought you'd just neglected to shower or use deodorant or whatever. I kept getting whiffs of damp fur and mud mixed in with Nina's bite-sized Snickers."

Teddy fought the impulse to sniff her armpits. She'd showered today…

Nina rose now, too, towering over Teddy. At five-seven, she'd never felt so small. The woman's nostrils flared, but she shook her head. "That means Katniss Tranquilizer Gun here is paranormal, too. So what are you and why can't anyone define you by your fucking scent? Shit, I hope it's something new. I'm damn tired of vampires and werewolves."

Teddy stretched her neck upward, shoving her hands inside the pockets of her down vest. No backing down, no matter how big and scary. And if Nina was anything, she was intimidating. Yet there was a hint of vulnerability to her Teddy didn't understand.

"What are *you?*"

Nina rolled her tongue in her cheek, squinting one almond-shaped eye as she cocked her head. "Former vampire."

That explained the discontent she'd sensed earlier. "Former?"

"Long fucking story, part of the reason we're here. Now ante up or I'll have you breathing through your belly button in ten seconds flat."

"So you're officially human now? No super vampire powers to speak of?"

"Yeah."

"Then I'd like to see you try."

Nina's gaze was straight on and deadlocked on Teddy's face. Her posture changed, her body language riddled with tension so real, she was like a bow ready to snap an arrow off. "Correct me if I'm fucking wrong, but am I hearing a challenge from your ruby-red lips?"

"You're hearing my defense in regards to your threat. I like breathing from my mouth, thank you."

Marty grabbed at Nina's arm, dragging her out of her imposing stance. "This is exactly what I mean. You no longer have the muscle to back up the claims, bully! If you keep this up, you're going to get us all killed one day. Do you want this to end the way it did with that poor man Eddie in the parking lot of the Dollar Store?"

Nina rolled her eyes in response, shaking Marty off. "Oh, fuck off. He deserved to have his shit handed to him. He was parked in a damn wheelchair parking spot. I just told him so."

"No. That's not the entire story. He was picking up his elderly mother, Mad Dog. He almost took your head off with a tire iron when you went at him like some sort of raging bull, Nina! And now that you're human, a guy the size of a fully stocked fridge can do you some serious harm. You made me make him doubt his manhood after I got done sticking up for you. In front of his mother!" she howled in outrage. "Now for the last time, back the hell off, and stop trying to fill a role you no longer fit the requirements for!"

This particular admission left Teddy with instant remorse. How odd would it be to lose the part of her that had its own way of life? To lose the people closest to her because she didn't have the same needs, the same abilities, the same struggles they did? It had to be like an average student ending up in the class for Mensa members.

Nina was struggling. With this huge change in her life, with her friends' resistance to the changes, with the inability to live on the same plane they did.

She knew diddly squat about vampires—even less about how a vampire could possibly be a vamp one minute and human the next. But she regretted her rude words.

Instantly she turned to Nina, placing a hand on Marty's shoulder to indicate she should back off her friend. "It's okay, Marty. Really. I'm sorry, Nina. That was rude of me. I apologize."

Nina flapped an irritated hand at her, slung her backpack over her shoulder and stomped to the farthest corner of the cabin where a small kitchen and a sink with actual running water was located. She dragged a misshapen wooden stool from the corner and plopped down into it, essentially turning her back on everyone.

Crap.

"So what are you?" Cormac finally spoke, his voice slithering over her like a sensual bath of silky warm water.

Her eyes met his, head on without blinking. "I'm a bear. Just like you. Brown bear, if you're interested."

Nina had that twinkle in her eye when she made scary bear paws. "You mean like roar, and shredding-unsuspecting-fucking-campers-while-they-roast-marshmallows, stealing-honey-from-hives, raw-fish-eating, *Goldilocks-and-The-Three-Bears* bear?"

Under any other circumstance, she would have laughed. "Mostly that's what I mean. Except for the raw fish. Just can't do it."

"You've shredded unsuspecting campers?" Cormac asked.

Teddy looked right at him. "Duh. Don't all bears? Is there anything better than hearing, 'Oh my God, please don't eat me, you mean, vicious bear!' as you rip their throats out and collect your booty of baked beans and kerosene lanterns?"

"Aren't you a real standup comedienne? You do The Improv when you're done eating people?" Cormac returned.

"Okay, so wait. Lemme get this shit right. Your name is *Teddy*?" The former vampire squeaked her name out on a high note.

Did high school ever really end? "I know. Irony, right? Theodora/Teddy equals ha-ha-ha."

Nina's head fell back, revealing her slender throat. "Buwhahahhaha! Oh, Christ on a cracker, that's the best shit I've heard in forever!"

"Wait, you're a bear, too?" Wanda gasped out at Cormac. "Are you sure you're the Cormac Vitali who has a sister from Jersey about yeah-high, gorgeous red hair, feisty as a coon who's been cornered in a crawl space, with the heart of a warrior?"

Teddy noted his eyes were less narrow now, more contemplative. "I'm sure."

"So does someone want to explain to me why Toni wouldn't tell us you were a bear? We spent a solid month with her in Shamalot—"

"What the hell is Shamalot?" Cormac asked, once more crossing his arms over his wide chest.

"It's a very, very long story. One we'd be happy to share with you. *Privately*," Wanda added with a direct gaze in Teddy's vicinity. "But that still doesn't answer the question. Why would Toni purposely not tell us you're a bear? Why isn't she a bear, too?"

His answer was stiff as he rose and moved to his computers, turning each screen off. "Because she didn't know. It happened after we…"

After what?

Teddy wanted to ask, but he wasn't at all approachable at this point. She needed to get a call in to her brothers and figure out where everything had gone so wrong.

"Can we speak somewhere privately, Cormac? We have a lot to discuss," Wanda reminded him again, pointing to a door just beside the small kitchen.

Cormac eyed her with suspicion as he pulled off his knit cap and lobbed it on the makeshift plywood he used as a desk. "And *her?*"

Teddy fought an angry retort, opting to remain silent. Her was just fine, thank you very much.

"I'll stay with her," Marty offered, rolling up her sleeves as though she were preparing to babysit a T-Rex. "She can tell me all about this life mate thing while you two talk."

Like she needed a babysitter. But there was no getting out of this now. She was in for the duration. At least until she could get a phone call to her brothers.

And until she could figure out what to do about this call her heart had made.

Because whether Cormac Vitali liked it or not, he was destined to be hers.

* * *

Cormac sat on a hard chair opposite Wanda, who'd taken a spot on the bed, crossing her legs as she explained to him this completely whacked tale of wormholes, knights and princes and ogres and Toni, who was, if he'd heard correctly, planning to marry a prince and would thus be a princess, and living in an entirely different realm.

He calmly stroked his cat, Lenny Kravitz's ears while he listened, and Lenny purred with contentment.

"Are you hearing everything I'm saying, Cormac? Did you hear me tell you I'm a hybrid, or as my dear friend calls me, a halfsie?"

Yep. Half vampire, half werewolf. He'd heard.

"Oh, I hear you talking."

"But have you absorbed what I've said?"

"Like the proverbial sponge."

She sighed a grating, impatient sound he was meant to hear and shifted her position on the shabby quilt he'd pulled up over his pillow just this morning. She looked almost out of place in a room so sparse and dim compared to her refined sophistication. She belonged with fine crystal, silk drapes and fancy goblets in a mansion somewhere.

Her voice took on a stern teacher's tone when she said, "I'm not the enemy here, Cormac. So I'd appreciate it if you'd kindly stop treating me as such and pay me the respect I deserve for hauling my butt up this damn mountain just to find you. I came all the way here from New York because we made a promise to your sister—someone we hold quite dear to our hearts after all we've been through. If you're not willing to listen to me, then I'm happy to leave you right here in your frozen tundra of a prison. I do have a family and things that need tending back at home. I also have Nina. A very disgruntled, very lost ex-vampire who, as you've seen, is a beast with a food obsession. Clearly you can see my plate is full. Now, either you participate in this conversation, and squish your way onto my full plate, nestled in next to Nina the Crabby, or I leave you here with your alleged *life mate* and I go home."

Rolling his head on his neck, he stretched it from side to side, setting Lenny on the floor. Her story was insane.

But was it any more insane than the idea that he'd been bitten and turned into a bear by a Russian mob member? The hair that clogged the drain in that pitiful shower of his after one of those bone-crunching shifts certainly said otherwise.

"You have to admit it's a lot to wrap your brain around."

Her face relaxed then and her lips tilted upward in a small smile. "You heard the part about OOPS, our company, right?"

"The paranormal crisis hotline. Yep. I did." More crazy. Maybe. Then again, maybe not.

"Then you understand that absorbing these sorts of things is a steady diet for me and my friends."

"Okay, I get the paranormal bit. I do. I get the accident bit, too. But the other-realm thing—Shamalot? A prince? An ogre? Fairies? A *castle*?"

Her lovely face turned sour when she wrinkled her nose at him. "Is that really any more difficult to believe than you being accidentally bitten and turned into a bear? A *bear*? Please, Cormac. Surely you're past the stage of disbelief if you've been living with this for three years."

He rubbed the spot where his finger had once been and grimaced. "Point taken. Look, I know I'm being pretty ornery here, but I've been on guard day and night since this whole thing with Toni's ex-thug of a boyfriend went down. How am I supposed to just trust that you people even know Toni, let alone can help me when no one else will? Not the police, not anyone? I think it's only fair that if I have to see your side of things, you should have to at least take mine into consideration."

She slapped her thigh and finally smiled, lightening the vibe of the room in an instant. "Fair enough. But I do have proof we know Toni."

He sat up straight, wary but all ears. "Via a crystal ball straight from Castle Nantucket?"

Wanda pursed her lips, very clearly not enjoying the joke as she scooped Lenny up and rubbed her nose against his white head. "Castle Beckett, Funny Man. I'll let that slide for now and just tell you, I know something no one else but you and Toni and one other person in the world knows."

Now she had his attention—but… "How do I know you didn't beat it out of her? Maybe hack off her finger the way Stas and his goons hacked off mine to get her to talk?"

Wanda got that eye of the tiger again when she looked at him. "You don't. There's a modicum of trust we're going to have to lend each other here. Once you get to know me—know *us*—you'll see how utterly absurd that statement is regarding my two yappy friends and myself. But I also think you're going to have to take a stab at logic here. Why, if we wanted to kill you, aren't you already dead? *That*, you can either take or leave." She smoothed her hand over her snow pants and re-crossed her legs, cool as a cucumber, and waited.

According to some of those ebooks he'd read, he should at least be able to sense whether she was being truthful. But that's what he got for putting stock in romance novels because they were the only pseudo guide on the web with anything even remotely like his own very real-life trauma. His choices had turned out to be very slim.

Leaning back, now Cormac crossed his feet at his ankles as Lenny wound his tail around them and said, "Okay, show me your proof."

"You have a tattoo."

Cormac lifted an eyebrow, keeping his face passive. "Do I?"

"You do. Toni told us she only knows about it because your best friend Damon never lets you live down that night of infamy and takes every opportunity to razz you about it."

Shit. Maureen. Aka Mo. His first love. The first love he'd lost, and after seven or eight beers, he'd drunkenly memorialized his love for her with a tattoo. With all sorts of declarations about how he'd never love anyone the way he loved Mo, he'd demanded his friend, Damon, take him to a tattoo parlor where he had her name glorified in ink.

On his left ass cheek.

"And what do you know about Damon and this tattoo?"

"I know it's your ex-girlfriend's name on your left butt cheek and you got it in a drunken tattoo parlor run after Mo broke up with you."

That still didn't prove anything. "How do I know you didn't force Toni to tell you something so personal?"

"Are you denying Mo's name is on your ass?"

He squirmed in his chair at the memory of that damn night when he was just twenty-one and drunk on what he was sure was love. "I can neither confirm nor deny."

"Then I believe we're done. Now, do you want help catching Stas and having him thrown in jail, where he can rot for eternity, so you can see your sister again? Or would you prefer we take our leave?"

Suddenly, he didn't know. He was so busy keeping his guard up, so used to being alone, aside from the fact that he was unsure they were telling the truth, he didn't know if he could even accept help anymore. Besides, how could these women help him catch someone who had the entire Jersey police department in his pocket?

"Surely, as those wheels in your mind turn, you're not doubting our ability to help you, are you? It was *you* I took down like a tree in the forest, wasn't it?"

Now he gave her a sheepish grin. "You're pretty tough. I'll let you have that."

"Times two if you include Marty. Add in the other forces we have at work for us, and we're a pretty damn good team to have on your side. I wish Nina could help as well, but like I said…" She sighed forlornly. "Marty wasn't joking when she was taunting Nina about chewing her face off. Nina was a formidable foe."

"So you were all accidently bitten?"

Wanda had explained how they'd all come to be, something he couldn't deny because of his situation, but certainly something that would take time to digest.

She bobbed her head and chuckled. "Every last one of us, and we help people who've had the same experience all the time through OOPS."

He'd kept his poker face on when Teddy had declared herself a bear, but this was unreal. Now he found himself riddled with curiosity; to know there were others just like him was incredible. "Was Nina always so testy?" The question slipped out before he was able to contain it.

Wanda's expression was one of pride, despite her next words. "You mean before she was bitten? She was a horror. But she was pretty tough even without the vampire thing. She's always been cranky and difficult. She has no filter. She's very confrontational. But as a vampire? She was a bloody warrior with no fear and no doubt she'd come out on top of whatever we faced. Alas, she always did come out on top…"

Wanda's voice sounded so gloomy, it left his chest feeling tight, though he couldn't quite explain why. Maybe because they'd both shared a huge loss? The losses were nothing alike, but they were still losses.

"So how did she become human again?"

She lifted her chin, her glossed lip trembling ever so slightly before she appeared to mentally shake it off. "She saved your sister from a very powerful, crazed Queen in Shamalot named Angria. Nina threw herself in the face of this queen's rage and sank her teeth into her neck to keep her from killing Toni, who was only trying to save the man she'd fallen in love with," she said in a hushed tone.

Cormac swallowed, unable to speak. He'd come so close to losing Toni not just once, but twice? He closed his eyes and tried to gather his thoughts. If Wanda was lying, she was damn good at it. To come to him with a story as outlandish as this Shamalot tale was one thing. That alone took an act of pure faith, not to mention courage.

But to then concoct a story about this Nina saving Toni's life and losing her vampiric powers in the process would be beyond ballsy.

"And Theodora?" he asked, her very name on his lips feeling foreign yet comfortable. "Do you think she's a part of this thing with Stas?"

Wanda sucked in her cheeks again, taking a deep breath. "I don't know, Cormac. I can't get a clear read on her. So we keep her close until we know differently."

To trust Wanda or not.

That was the question.

The other question was the gorgeous summer-blonde lunatic in the other room. Sure, most guys would be happy to have a woman as beautiful as Theodora "Teddy" Jackson declare them hers.

However, a hot woman and a mate for life were two different things, according to those romance novels.

So what to do about the beautiful blonde with the curvy hips, long legs, raspberry-tinted full lips and startlingly hazel eyes. A woman who smelled like Nirvana wrapped in the meaning of life.

Whoa-whoa-whoa. Why was he espousing her attributes when he thought she was batshit?

Why can't she be one donut hole shy of a dozen and hot? Is there a rule against it? Some unwritten law none of us are aware of, Pooh Bear?

But wait. Wasn't this the way every single one of those relationships in romance novels had begun?

One of the protagonists declaring an unwitting, sometimes unwilling partner their life mate? They fight, they have all kinds of sexual tension, they have some sort of inner conflict, coupled with an external conflict that keeps them apart, but in the end they overcome said obstacles, fall madly in love and mate?

No. That was crazy made-up shit.

Yep. Just like all the other crazy made-up shit, Mr. Bear.

Well, hell.

Chapter 4

"So life mate, huh? I had no idea bears even had life mates," Marty prodded, skepticism lacing her tone as she poured Teddy some tea she'd found by rummaging in a cabinet.

She was as uncomfortable hearing it as she was admitting it. But for the time being, the explanation had saved her hide and kept her from showing all her cards. "We do."

"What happens in your community if you don't mate with your alleged life mate? Do you have alphas and such who enforce the mate?"

Teddy sipped her tea and eyed Marty over the rim of her mug, weighing her options. But she remembered the rule about inviting anyone into their private culture. Even if Marty and the others were paranormal, they weren't bears.

"Do you mean like a leader? Like packs and clans and stuff?"

"Packs, clans, a murder of crows, a herd of dust bunnies. Whatever."

"We're called sleuths, and no. We don't have a leader, per se. We don't band together in quite the way I've heard your kind does." After defining their paranormal roles, Teddy had a much clearer picture of what she was dealing with.

She'd never met a vampire or a werewolf or an ex-paranormal anything, but she'd heard rumors about their kind, understood the basic inner workings of their mating rituals.

"So what happens if you won't mate with your intended—or you can't get your intended to mate with you? Do they turn you into a rug?" She laughed at her own joke then, the tinkle of it grating on Teddy's frayed nerves. Somehow, she had to get away from these women and call her brothers, pronto.

Clarity was desperately needed. Cormac was a bad guy, but if what she'd felt when he'd looked into her eyes was true—if the legend meant anything at all—he was *her* bad guy.

But he's a criminal, Teddy…

Of course he is. Why would finding her honest-to-God life mate be any easier than anything else in her life when it came to relationships? Remember the last one and how that turned out?

Stirring her tea, Teddy forced a laugh. "It's frowned upon, but not necessarily enforced. Plenty of bears mate with bears who aren't necessarily considered their traditional life mates. But the rule of thumb is probably much like yours. You know the score where that's concerned. Procreate for the good of the group, yadda, yadda, yadda."

Marty leaned forward, pressing her chin into her fist, her eyes glittering. "So how did you know your life mate was here? Somewhere so secluded, even remote? Denver's pretty far away. Was it intuition? A dream? Tea leaves?"

Teddy looked past Marty to Nina's back, where she focused her gaze as she lied once more. "Instinct, I guess." Not a total lie. Her instincts had helped her locate Cormac, she just didn't know at the time he was her life mate.

"You're awfully vague, aren't you?" Marty said in the most pleasant of ways, yet there was the underlying subtext of her suspicion in every word.

She'd purposely kept her answers vague. The less she lied, the less she had to recall. "It's a little personal, I suppose."

Nina swiveled around on her chair and made a face, licking her thumb clean of the remaining salt from her potato chips. "Vague means get off the broad's back and mind your own damn beeswax, Marty. Jesus and the moose lodge. It's not your job to figure out the direction her hormones are pointed or anything else that has to do with her. That's not why we're here."

Score one for the ex-vampire Nina. She was proving useful.

But Marty waved her off in a dismissive flick of her hand. "It's just girl talk, Nina. Something you'd know nothing about."

The undercurrent of anger in Marty's words gave Teddy pause. Why was she so angry with Nina and why did she care? But it gave her the opportunity to divert the conversation. "So why are *you* all here?"

Marty's pink-glossed lips instantly thinned, though she quickly slapped a phony smile on and a wide-eyed expression of innocence graced her face. "Just visiting."

Now Teddy was suspicious. Tucking her hair behind her ears, she stuck her toe in the deep end of the pool. "It didn't sound like Cormac knew you…"

"He's a friend of a friend."

Nina's chair scraped abruptly against the floor. "Look, *Teddy*, here's the score. We don't know you and you don't know us. It's none of your damn business how we know the big dude or why we're here. So let's quit pussyfootin' around until we figure this out and someone tells us we have to be one big happy paranormal family, okay?"

Marty groaned, dropping her head into her hands. "Nina. Don't be so rude."

"Aw, fuck you and your rude. I'm still just as sick and tired of pretense as I ever was. Even more tired of the cat-and-mouse bullshit we play every time we run into someone with secrets. And you got secrets, *Theodora*. I damn well know you do. I'm just not that interested in 'em. So if you don't want to tell us your secrets, we're not gonna ask about 'em. But that means you can't ask about ours either. Cormac's with us and he's not goin' anywhere without us from now until we say other-fucking-wise. So deal with your own shit and we'll deal with ours. *Capisce?*"

That had gone south fast. And she sure as shit did have secrets. Still, the hell she was laying all her cards on the table before she knew if these women were bad guys, too.

"So the pajama party is off?" she joked, knowing full well it would get under Nina's skin.

"Yep. And so is braiding your hair and doing your fucking nails. Got it?"

Rising from her chair, Teddy held her head high and reached for her vest. "Loud and clear. Now, if you ladies don't mind, I have to make a phone call. I have family waiting to hear from me and I can't seem to get a signal inside the cabin. Is that all right, or do you want to babysit me outside, too?"

"Fuck that. It's a million below out there in the tundra," Nina groused, rubbing her long arms with her hands.

She looked to Marty, who'd also risen, for permission to leave the premises.

Marty gave her a short nod and a no-nonsense gaze. "Stay within sight and keep in mind, I'm a werewolf. We're slicker n' snot. I imagine we're much faster than a bear. I can and will outrun you, Teddy. Also note: I have big, ugly, drooly teeth. I'll use them. Don't go far."

Without a word, Teddy made her way out of the kitchen and toward the purple door, swinging it open while trying to keep her cool.

Once outside, she stomped through the snow toward the clothesline, right in Marty's line of vision, where she could watch Teddy from the window by the door, but she hoped far enough away to go unheard. Digging her cell phone from the back pocket of her jeans, she held it up, hoping to get a signal.

If she'd lied about most everything else, she hadn't lied about not being able to get a single bar on her phone.

With shaking fingers, she scrolled her screen and almost cheered when she saw the bars light up. Hitting autodial, she called Vadim, praying he wasn't off somewhere on the ranch.

Just as the line began to ring, she caught movement from the left side of the cabin. A rustle of fallen leaves, the very slight crunch of snow.

Instantly, Teddy crouched, tucking her body so she managed to stay out of sight. The scent of cigarette smoke whispered under her nose. Smoke and sweat.

How strange. No one in the cabin smelled of smoke…

She decided to investigate. Turning her phone to silent, she slipped it back in her pocket and dove for a path Cormac must have dug from the side of the cabin to the front pathway. He'd piled the sides high enough with snow that she'd be able to observe without being seen. Rolling to her side, she scrambled to her haunches, shook off the snow and crouched down to assess.

Her heart began to throb in her chest for no apparent reason. Something wasn't right. She felt it. Smelled it. Knew it deep in her gut.

Poking her head over the snowbank, Teddy narrowed her gaze, sniffing the air to recapture the scent of the cigarette and focusing in on the location it came from.

A hunter maybe? Who hunted at night…and wasn't this part of the forest preserved? A poacher? The son of a bitch. Was he a poacher looking for illegal pelts?

And that was when she finally located him. A dark, bulky figure, hunched over by a pile of freshly cut wood, holding a sniper rifle.

Hold the phone. A *sniper rifle?* What kind of hunter used a sniper rifle? Or was this guy here for the women? Or worse, Cormac?

Was he out here for someone else? Another inhabitant of the cabin maybe? Maybe they were looking for this Toni they were all talking about?

Craning her neck, Teddy slid silently down along the bank of snow until she had a better view of the guy. That was when she saw the laser site, gleaming and red.

She had to keep herself from scoffing at how amateur a laser site on a sniper rifle was.

Sissy.

And then she saw *whom*, not what, he was aiming for. The red beam flashed at the window of the cabin as he lined up his mark.

Her eyes flew open and her hands broke out into a clammy sweat. His mark was Cormac.

Dread filled the pit of her stomach, her heart crashed so hard, it was likely to fall out of her chest. What kind of shit was her life mate into?

Tall and strong, Cormac stood right in front of the streaked glass pane, talking to Wanda, who was over his shoulder as he sipped a beer with the light from the site aimed right at his heart.

Holy hell, he was aiming for Cormac.

Without thinking of anything other than stopping whoever it was with their finger on the trigger from killing Cormac, she launched over the snow bank, head down, mouth wide open.

"Cormac, duuuuuuck!" Teddy hollered as she landed by the front door with a grunt before tucking and rolling. Scrambling to her feet, she heard the gun go off just above her head, pinging what sounded like metal.

There was no time to think as she made a break to the left side of the cabin, crawling her way toward the pile of wood where the shooter was located.

Shots fired, zigzagging and pinging off every area of the cabin, becoming more erratic with each bullet. Someone wanted him dead, and they wanted him dead *bad*.

She had nothing to defend herself with, no weapon to speak of, but clearly she had to do something because this moron wasn't leaving without Cormac.

There was all manner of yelling and carrying on coming from inside the cabin as chaos ensued. Someone yelled her name, but she ignored it in favor of catching this son of a bitch who'd dared to take a shot at the man she was destined to spend the rest of her life with—despite the fact that they knew absolutely nothing about one another, and Cormac was an alleged bad guy.

He continued to shoot wildly at the cabin, which suggested desperation on the sniper's part. Something she didn't understand. Unless…

There was no time to figure out his motivation. He was taking potshots with careless abandon—someone was going to end up hurt.

Grabbing one of the freshly chopped logs, she peered into the velvety night, found her victim, and with a grunt of a cry, lobbed the heavy piece of wood directly at his head.

It slammed into the side of his skull with a satisfying *thunk*, but it didn't take him out. Not by a long shot. Instead, it made him angrier.

"Teddy! Where the hell are you?" Marty cried, barreling out the door and directly into the fray.

Just as the werewolf poured out of the cabin, Cormac and Wanda followed suit, with Nina on the fringe, and they were headed directly in the path of the shooter.

"Nina, stay in the cabin before you get yourself killed!" Wanda screamed.

She had to do something, and do it fast.

So she did the only thing she knew to do. Charge the son of a bitch and pray all those old tires she'd jumped through over and over while her brothers trained her had done a good job of teaching her how to bob and weave.

Threading her way toward the man with the gun, she ducked in an erratic pattern, moving in and out of the shadows as she heard the shooter begin to retreat. His footsteps were easily identifiable just up ahead, heavy and clunky; he tore his way toward the hill.

With his back to her, Teddy decided, it was now or never. No way was she letting this guy go so he could roam freely, and chance he might come back for round two at another time.

With a guttural growl, Teddy launched herself at his back, aiming for the dark coat he wore with the sole purpose of knocking him to the ground and finding out who the hell he was.

She hit him with a bone-crunching thud, her body bouncing on his spine, his gun getting air and dropping out of his grasp before she pinned him and grabbed him by a thatch of his greasy hair, dragging his head upward so she could get a good look at his face.

"Who the hell are you?" she roared down at him.

He paused for only a moment, a brief, eerily suspended moment, before he smiled and held up a gleaming knife, jamming it into her side.

Her scream ripped from her throat when the knife sliced into her like a hot poker, searing her flesh. A scream of horror, defeat, pure rage emitted from somewhere deep within her chest. Blood began to gush from her side, warm and sticky, the scent coppery and thick.

The shooter tossed her off as though she weighed no more than a feather, leaving her in a gasping lump on the cold ground.

But she'd seen the son of a bitch.

And he looked just like one of the mug shots she'd seen on Cormac's computer screen before he'd shut them down.

* * *

Cormac scooped Teddy up as gently as possible, brushing her hair from her face as the women twittered around him.

"I can walk," she said with a protest, trying to lift out of the cradle of his arms.

"I bet. You can also bleed," he murmured back. "You're making a pretty big mess, you know."

"I'll try harder to keep my bleeding on the inside the next time I chase after a guy who's trying to kill you. Care to explain what that was about?" She hissed the words while trying to reposition herself to ease the sting of her wound.

Cormac looked her directly in the eye and shook his head, his beautiful lips moving in precise motion. "Nope."

"You do know life mates share everything, don't you?" She went for the joke in the hopes he'd bite.

"I know no such thing." He continued to crunch through the snow, keeping her tight to his chest.

Okay, he wasn't biting. Fine. There'd be time for warm-fuzzies and long walks on the beach later. For now, someone was trying to kill Cormac.

Why the fuck was someone trying to kill Cormac? There'd been no mention of anyone else hunting him…

Marty's face appeared to her right, masked in worry, her blue eyes wide. "Oh my God, Teddy! You ran right after him like you were part of the SWAT team! It was incredible—and plum nuts. He could have killed you."

She waved Marty off. If she only knew the half of what she'd run into, around, over and under in order to make some cash. "I'm fine. Promise. I heal pretty quickly. Maybe not as quickly as you ladies do, but fairly fast. It'll pass."

"That was absolutely crazy, Theodora Jackson, and you'd better never do it again on my watch," Wanda ordered as she grabbed her fingers and gave them a squeeze.

Nina greeted them at the door, holding it open and pointing to the couch with mismatched cushions. "Put Rambo's ass there. I'll clean her up."

Cormac set Teddy down on the surface with careful hands while Wanda and Marty plumped a throw pillow behind her and settled her in.

"Do you have a first-aid kit, dude?" Nina asked Cormac, wincing when she saw the blood at Teddy's side.

He pointed to the cabinet in the kitchen while Wanda and Marty made her raise her arms so they could peel her jacket off and lift her shirt up.

As they peeled her shirt from her skin, she hissed her pain, biting back a scream of agony. Fuck that hurt, and if she ever caught the bastard who'd knifed her in the gut, she was going to rip his heart out by digging her way inside his chest with a goddamn spoon.

Nina pushed her way into the fray, settling between Teddy's knees, first-aid kit in hand. "Fuck all if that's not deep, kiddo. Marty, get me some hot water, a cloth and some of that booze Yogi Bear's hiding under the sink."

Had Nina's tone changed? Was that concern in her voice? Teddy was certain it was worry.

What happened to "you deal with your shit and I'll deal with mine"?

Marty brought all the items and set them on the floor by Nina's feet. The ex-vampire grabbed the bottle of Jack and dumped it on a cloth. "This shit's gonna hurt like a fucking bitch. Ten bucks and a bag of my gummi bears says you scream."

Teddy sucked in a breath, her toes curling inside her boots. "You're on, and if you just give it a chance to heal—"

"It's still gotta be cleaned, moron. What if something slows up the healing? You wanna wander around with your intestines gushing outta your side? I've been hurt a time or twenty. I think I know what I'm talking about."

If only Nina knew how often she'd been roughed up. Never stabbed, mind you, but beat to hell and left needing stitches? Hell yeah. "Fine," she gritted out. "Just do it."

"Hold her arms, ladies—this is gonna sting," Nina ordered Marty and Wanda, tucking her long hair behind her ear before she pressed the cloth to Teddy's side.

Just a blip of a second before she nearly skyrocketed off the couch from the sting, she felt the lightest of touches, a mere wisp of Cormac's fingertips glancing hers. Calloused and rough, he wrapped them around her digits and squeezed.

And then Teddy fought a scream of anguish—because no way was she losing ten bucks—digging her heels into the hard floor, almost biting her tongue off to keep from crying out.

Nina eyeballed her from where she was hunched on the floor in front of her and winked her approval.

And for some crazy, weird reason, as sweat formed on her upper lip and she almost burst every blood vessel in her head to stay quiet, Teddy was ridiculously pleased this grumpy, mean, no-bullshit ex-vampire approved of her stiff upper lip—and Cormac held her hand through it all.

Chapter 5

Cormac watched Teddy sip a hot toddy Marty had mixed for her, the sight of her lickable lips curling over the rim of the mug making him warm all over.

Jesus. This was such bullshit. How could he feel anything for a woman he didn't even know? Yet, when he'd seen Teddy charge that guy, somewhere deep in his chest, a small piece of him dislodged, broke off, reattached itself and made a home under his skin, where this alarming emotion made itself comfortable.

Well, you know, that one romance novel you read said this is how life mates react to one another. You just know instinctually that person is your person. Remember? You were up until four in the morning reading all about it, Casanova.

He remembered. He'd thought it was bullshit then and he thought exactly that now.

Then why is your heart beating faster? Why do you want to ask her all sorts of stupid questions? Like if she had a date for her senior prom. What her favorite sleeping position is. If she puts ketchup or mustard on her hot dogs.

If she puts ketchup on her hot dog, it's over. Mustard all the way. Spicy brown, thank you very much.

Stop, you silly. It's only just begun. You won't care if she doesn't brush her teeth or scratches her metaphorical balls. You're in, pal. You're just shy of twirling your hair and batting your eyelashes.

Clearing his throat, Cormac sat up on the recliner across from the couch and forced himself to be involved in this conversation about the sniper. "So you're sure this guy was aiming at me?" he asked, Teddy.

Brushing her hair from her face, she bobbed her head. "One hundred percent. He had a site on a sniper rifle with a red laser beam. It was aimed at your chest via the bedroom window. So why don't you tell me what's going on here? How many people have a hit man after them? I think at the very least I deserve an explanation."

Because she'd put herself in the line of fire for him, was the not-so-subtle implication.

Wanda looked at him, sending him some kind of signal he didn't understand in what he supposed was girl-speak. It probably meant shut up. So rather than run the risk of saying too much, he remained in stubborn silence.

Teddy slid to the edge of the couch, her wound obviously feeling better. "Better yet, why don't you tell me why the guy I tackled out there while I was keeping him from killing you looked just like one of the men you had up on your screen when we first got to the cabin?"

Cormac fought to keep his face nonreactive, but his pulse began that harsh bounce in his neck. "A guy on the screen?"

Fuck all, they'd found him. Fuck, fuck, fuck all.

Teddy rolled her eyes to let him know he wasn't fooling anyone. "Yeah, the guy with the scruffy dark beard, beady black eyes, who looks like he bathes once every full moon cycle and goes by the name of Andre, if I caught it right before you turned the computer off. What is it you don't want me to see?"

Shit. She *had* seen. Andre was one of Stas's goons. One of the motherfuckers responsible for hacking off his finger.

So Andre had finally come to take him out, which meant Stas and whomever he worked for had found him and decided his time on earth was due to come to an end.

Fuck. How the hell had they found him after all this time?

He liked it here. It was as close to safe as he'd felt in the three years he'd been on the run.

So he played dumb. "You're sure it was the same guy?"

Teddy's eyes narrowed in suspicion as she set the mug down and folded her hands together, her slender fingers curling into a ball. "I already said it was. So who is Andre and why does he want you dead?"

Because he works for my sister's psychopath ex-boyfriend and I know sensitive information about him. What was the right answer here? What if Teddy worked for these murderers?

That makes absolutely no sense. She would have just let Andre take you out and skipped on down the mountain all sexy and sassy. She sure as hell wouldn't have let him knife her in the gut for you just for show, fool.

His eyes went to Wanda, who clucked her tongue and intervened. "You saw *his* face. Did he see yours, Teddy?"

"Well, yeah," she scoffed with a snort. "I was on top of him, demanding who he was. Looked right at me before he jammed the knife in my side."

Nina smiled on a grunt as she nudged Teddy's shoulder with her own. She held up her fist for a bump. "You are one bad muthafluffin' bitch. Gimme one."

Teddy grinned for the first time then, and it was exquisite. The upward turn of her lips changed the map of her face entirely as she fist-bumped with Nina, punching him hard in the gut with more feels.

Stop getting the cuddlies over Teddy. She could well be the enemy.

Make up your damn mind. You can't have it both ways. Either I allow the warm-fuzzies to take hold or I think of her as a foe.

"Okay, that means we're absolutely not safe here," Wanda reminded. "First, this Andre is still wandering around out there, maybe waiting to take another shot at us. Second, he's seen Teddy, which means she's not safe either."

Teddy held up a hand, rising from the couch with purpose. "Hold up now. Obviously this guy is a bad dude. And now he's seen me. If I didn't deserve to know why he was after Cormac before, I damn well do now. Now I'm in danger, too. But from *what*? Somebody better start talking before I take myself back down this mountain and find the local authorities."

That's more than fair, man, and you know it.

He opened his mouth for only a moment before Wanda intervened again when she rose and addressed them all with that air of authority she was so good at. "How about we do this instead. It's painfully obvious we can't stay here any longer. Andre is wild and free out there and he's seen both Cormac and Teddy. So let's go back home, where I know we can keep you safe."

"You're from New York," Teddy said. "I can't go to New York. I have family who'll worry. A job. A—"

"A life you hope to keep? A family you don't want to endanger?" Wanda asked, her eyebrows furrowing on her smooth forehead.

Teddy conceded with a sheepish admission, driving her hands into the pockets of her bloodied vest, "Okay, that's fair. But *New York?*"

"Yes, New York. Stop saying it like it's the Andes, for the love of Pete," Wanda chided. "We'll do our best to get this over and done with as soon as possible and you'll be right back here in Colorado before you can say pic-i-nic basket."

"If I'm going to New York, I at least deserve to know what the hell is going on!"

Cormac heard the rise of panic in Teddy's voice, saw the bright patches of crimson on her cheeks, and found he wanted to ease her fear. "I promise I'll explain everything when we get there, Teddy. But we don't really have a choice at this point. Please come with us. I couldn't live with myself if you were hurt again because of me." There. He'd said it. That was the truth.

Her face went from panicked to pacified in seconds, but she only nodded her agreement.

Wanda's nod was brisk. "Good enough. Nina, call Archibald—tell him we're headed to the castle and we need him to meet us there. Then call Darnell and ask him to contact Keegan to arrange the private plane. Tell him we have company. It's time to end this once and for all."

Both Teddy and Cormac looked to Wanda and simultaneously muttered with disbelief, "The *castle?*"

Wanda lifted her chin, her conservative yet chic stud earrings catching the light of the fire. "Are bears prone to hearing issues? I said castle. What about 'castle' don't the two of you understand?"

And a plane. Somebody named Keegan had a private plane?

Cormac couldn't help himself. He snorted. "Is it like that Castle Wicket you told me about?"

"It's *Beckett*, fuckwad," Nina spat at him just before she headed for the door. "Ease up on the sarcasm or I'll force-feed you some of that shit with a spoon. Don't even consider takin' cheap shots at where we been. Because I will fuck you up."

Wanda planted her hands on her hips, sizing them all up. "Are we going to put up a fight and ask a ridiculous amount of questions here? Because I'm just going to remind you again how fed up I am at this point when everyone questions my decisions. I've led this crew into more than one battle, and I've led them successfully. All while they bitch, they moan, they argue. But not this time, ladies and gents. Either you're in or you're out, and you'll decide without a single word of dissent. I'm not discussing it. I'm not fighting with any one of you about it.

"Cormac, you're not safe here. If you wish to be safe elsewhere, then follow me and I'll be sure Darnell handles any evidence you were ever anywhere near here. If not, let Andre make your unusually large body resemble a hunk of Swiss cheese. Teddy? I assume, since Cormac is your alleged life mate, you'll want to go with because as his *furever* girl, you want nothing but his safety. Now, we all assemble outside in five. If you're not there when I'm ready to get the hell off this mountain, then God-freakin'-speed!"

Wanda pivoted on her heel then, sauntering to the door and pulling it open as the frigid night air whooshed in and she exited, her head held high.

Nina slapped a stunned Cormac on the back, the scent of Cool Ranch Doritos on her breath. "You heard her, Pooh Bear. If you want to get to the bottom of this shit, bust a move, brother."

"But all the research I've compiled over the years is on my computer," he muttered under his breath, even though he knew what Wanda was suggesting was the right thing. "We'll need it."

Marty squeezed his arm and gave him a small smile. "Darnell will be here any second. He's hard to explain, but trust me; he'll make sure everything's handled. Promise. Now, I think you've got like three minutes and twenty-seconds left. Don't dally," she said on a chuckle, tucking her chin into her scarf and scooting out behind Nina.

Both he and Teddy looked at each other, their eyes guarded.

He was the first to speak, when he said, "So, *life mate*, are you in or are you out?"

She raised her chin, the sharp line of her jaw glinting in the light of the roaring fireplace, her hazel eyes glittering. "And miss staying in a castle? My Disney princess dreams just exploded in my head. Oh, believe this. I'm all in, *life mate*. All in."

Cormac fought a chuckle as she made her way outside to join the others, keeping his eyes averted to avoid looking at her curvaceous backside.

"One minute and thirty-two, Pooh Bear!" Nina shouted.

He scooped up Lenny and took a long last glance around the place that had been his sanctuary for three years now. The place he'd hated and loved for all manner of reasons. It was sparse, he'd lived with only what he truly needed, making trips into the neighboring town in a disguise to gather supplies only when it was absolutely necessary.

He'd learned far more than he ever thought he'd need about survival. About fear. About loss. He'd licked his wounds here. Raged against the unfair, cruel world here. He'd shifted for the first time here. Dealt with this crazy metamorphosis without anyone to turn to for help.

And he'd survived. He'd thrived. There was a small part of him that would miss the solitude, the beauty of the purple twilight fading into an orange ball of sun when he greeted each new day. The wildflowers in the spring, the rush of the creek, the first fall of snow. The peaceful breeze, the soft scent of pine and lake water tickling his nose while he napped in the hammock he'd made out back.

But it was time to reclaim his life. Maybe not the old one he'd wanted—the one where he and Toni lived in neighboring towns and their children played together on his front lawn, and they celebrated births, graduations, had barbecues, went on vacations with their families together.

But something on par with all those things, all those dreams he'd left behind, would be really damn nice, even if it wasn't exactly what he'd fashioned in his mind.

And he was ready.

He was goddamned ready.

He'd actually miss this place he'd alternately called his prison and his home. But it was time to go. Cormac sucked in a deep breath of air and tucked Lenny into his down jacket. Focusing his eyes on the purple door he'd painted himself with an old can of paint he'd found in the closet, he opened it and strode outside to meet the others, and didn't look back.

* * *

Teddy finally spoke as they sat in Nina's castle living room, her mouth dry and her mind reeling. "So you're a demon?"

The enormous round man with high-top sneakers, gold chains and an NFL jersey, who looked more like a teddy bear than a servant of evil, nodded his scruffy dark head. "Yes, ma'am. Flyin' low under the radar o' hell like a boss."

Teddy was still trying to process everything. The castle, the baby vampini, Charlie—who Nina's husband Greg had whisked off to spend time at Wanda's house with her husband, Heath. The gentle zombie who went by the name of Carl, and brought her books and a blanket.

The freakin' hedge maze. She shook her head. A hedge maze. Nina had a hedge maze.

A demon that didn't want to eat your soul was almost too much. But a demon that looked like you could rest your head on his shoulder while you cried? Insanity.

"So you're a good demon?"

How could that be? Who *were* these people, with their weird cult-like group and a hotline for paranormal crisis called OOPS?

Darnell grinned, his teeth glowing in the dimly lit great room filled with all sorts of medieval paraphernalia and a velvet wall hanging of Barry Manilow back in his *Copacabana* days.

"Yep. Someday when all this has passed, you an' me, we'll sit a spell, maybe on Marty's big ol' porch swing, and I'll explain how that all happened. Right now, we gotta keep you and your mister safe."

Her mister. Hah. Did he mean the man who'd done nothing but give her the cold shoulder since they'd arrived in a blur of a flight on an amazing private jet with the word *Pack* on the side of it? That mister?

How did this life mate thing work anyway? Did Cormac feel it, too? Because if he did—if he felt this magnetic pull to her like she did to him—he was going to win an Oscar for hiding it on the outside.

She remembered a bit of the legend her mother had once told her a long time ago, but Masha Gribanov had been gone since she was fourteen…sixteen years now. Not a day went by when she didn't think about her mother, miss her, need her advice. If there was ever a moment she needed her, now was that time.

How could she possibly ask her brothers Vadim and Viktor about something as sensitive as life mates? They wouldn't know sensitive from a Costco-sized box of condoms.

Marty came and sat by her on the big red and gold couch made of beautiful brocade fabric, and patted her knee. "Glad you decided to join us."

"I'm just not sure what I'm joining you for."

Marty simply grinned, wiggling her fingers at Cormac's cat, Lenny Kravitz, who jumped into her lap and snuggled down. "But! You'll wake up tomorrow without a bullet between your eyes, and that's always a comfort, don't you think?"

Teddy swallowed hard. There wasn't much she was afraid of, but the unknown rated pretty high. "About that…"

Why did everyone know what was going on with this guy out in the woods but her?

"Oh, hell no. All answers and back story are up to your life mate to disclose, sister. I'm just here for the cheap thrills and Arch's weenies in a blanket."

Speaking of Arch—or Archibald, as he was introduced to her with much flourish—he'd once been a vampire and was now human, too.

Though, she had to admit, he was absolutely precious, from the top of his balding, British-accented head right down to the shoes that shone so bright, she saw her own reflection. His suit, silver ascot, and trousers were equally as immaculate. As Marty told it, he was Wanda and Heath's manservant, and a surrogate grandfather to the many paranormal children in this group of accidental friends.

Not to mention, he was, according to Nina, an amazing cook. The scents flying from the ultra-modern kitchen, where Nina had told her to make herself at home with anything in the enormous fridge but her chicken wings or she'd lose a kidney, were amazing.

Archibald held a tray of those very weenies in a blanket under her nose, the smell making her mouth water. It had been hours since she'd last eaten, and the grumble of her stomach said as much.

"Surely you're famished, Mistress Jackson? All that frigid mountain air and the call of the wild makes for a hearty appetite, yes?"

Despite the fact that she had not the first clue what she was doing here or why she'd agreed to come other than the fact that her heart, while still attempting to compartmentalize, told her she should be here, Teddy smiled up at him.

"Thank you, Archibald. This is very kind of you to cook on such short notice. I feel like we've been thrust upon you without warning."

His eyes gleamed down at her when he barked a laugh. "Bah! If you only knew how often the thrust happens, milady. Please, don't allow yourself to be troubled. There is no putting me out when it comes to a crisis. Everything is better when there are weenies in a blanket, wouldn't you agree?"

She popped one in her mouth, the flavors exploding on her tongue in a riot of such bliss, all she could do was nod with an emphatic bob of her head.

Arch beamed down at her, the wrinkles melting into the corners of his eyes. "Surely later we'll sit and chat. As for now, I must get to the kitchen and finish up the mini-quiches. It was all I could scrounge up at such a late hour."

Grabbing a few more of the delicacies, she dropped them on a napkin, ran her hand down along Lenny's back, and excused herself from Marty, heading straight for Cormac, who stood by the fireplace, his arm braced on the ornate mantle of Nina's great room.

He looked completely out of place in the more formal setting of Nina and Greg's castle and he still smelled dreadful. His faded jeans, torn at the knees, and black work boots had seen better days. The plaid red-and-black flannel shirt he wore beneath a black vest, fraying at the cuffs he'd rolled up to his elbows, was worn from use.

And still he was utterly breathtaking. His rugged good looks, his sinfully hot green eyes, his bulky body rippled with muscle, drew her like a moth to a flame.

Teddy approached with caution, luxuriating in the warmth of the fire.

"Weenie in a blanket for your thoughts?" she asked, keeping her voice light.

When his gaze met hers, Cormac asked a question in a tone that sounded like she owed him money. "Mustard or ketchup on your hot dogs?"

"Um, mustard. Spicy brown. You?"

"Same."

Her stomach rippled with delight. *Aw, how cute. You have something in common. Mustard on your trans-fatty acids.*

Then there was more awkward silence.

She inhaled and smiled up at him, hoping to encourage conversation. "Vanilla or chocolate?"

"Neither."

"You don't like ice cream? Who doesn't like ice cream?"

"Strawberry."

"Oh, phew! I was ready to pitch you to the curb before we got in too deep, life mate." Then she winced when she saw Cormac's jaw harden at the words life mate.

"Favorite side of the bed?" he asked, surprising her.

Her cheeks warmed. "Middle. I know. I'm a hog. Anyone I've ever slept with says so…" Ugh. Probably not a good idea to bring up past lovers and their sleeping arrangements. She sucked at small talk. "Sorry. That was insensitive."

He smiled for the first time—that smile that made her heart go pitter-pat. "It's okay. You're what, twenty-five? I can't expect you to have been celibate."

Now she blushed, sick with delight that he thought she was twenty-five. "Thirty, actually. How old are you?"

"Thirty-nine."

"So who's your sleuth?"

Cormac cocked his dark head, confusion in his glittering eyes. "My what?"

"Your sleuth. You know, your clan, your pack, your people?"

"Is that what they call a group of bears? I had no idea."

Now that was odd. Everyone who was anyone knew what fellow bears called one other. "That's what we've always called them. My sleuth, I mean."

"Who's we? Siblings?"

She grinned, thinking about her nitwit brothers. "Two. They're twins. Vadim and Viktor. Older by five years."

"Jackson?"

She stiffened, looking down at her napkin of weenies in a blanket. "Hmm?"

"Your last name is Jackson. Vadim and Viktor sound Russian. Are they?"

Oh damn. Why had she lied about her last name? "My mom was from Russia…"

Cormac nodded. "Ahhhh. Interesting. Ever been there?"

"Once when I was just a little kid. Really cool. Lots of ornate churches, borscht and everyone can do a triple axel."

He chuckled—a deep, resonant sound. "I bet."

"Your family?"

He paused, but only for a second. "One sister. Parents are gone now."

"Mine, too. I miss them."

"I get it. So you work at a wildlife refuge?"

He appeared to be warming to actually speaking to her, and though the sound of his voice made her utterly giddy, she was trying to keep that on the inside.

"Yeah. I love it. It's tough work sometimes, but more than worth the gratification it brings. I love animals and I especially love working with them." She slowed her roll for a moment, so as not to appear rambling. "So what do you do for a living?"

"Did. I was a coder for a big tech corporation in Jersey."

Teddy cocked her head, sensing his distress the moment he thought he'd said too much. "Did?"

His gaze found hers, searing her to the very spot she stood upon. "I left three years ago."

Three years? He hadn't worked in three years? Something, somewhere along the way, had gone very wrong. She absolutely had to talk to Viktor and Vadim.

"To move to the forests of Colorado? Was the reason behind that because of that guy Andre?"

End conversation. Cormac's yummy lips clamped shut, his thick muscles went rigid.

Teddy sighed, annoyed they kept playing this ridiculous game of I've Got A Secret, with no end in sight. "I get it. I went too far. Forgive me for trying to figure out what's going on when my life's in danger." She pivoted on her heel, preparing to go in search of someone who would actually engage in a conversation, when Cormac gripped her arm in a light hold.

The contact of his grip made her pulse race, but she kept her cool.

"I'm sorry. I promise I won't let anyone hurt you. But the story's long and complicated and we've known each other what, four or five hours? There's a modicum of trust we have to establish."

"All bets are off if my life's in danger, Cormac. I can't defend myself if I don't know what's going on. Screw trust." She shook him off and moved away from him.

Because you've told him everything, Teddy Bear? C'mon. Play fair here, girlie.

She had to make a phone call and she had to make one now. Nina had reassured her there were all manner of proper safety measures taken to keep them safe, like cell phone jammers and security systems she'd set when they went to bed. Which meant, she needed to get outside to make a call before the alarms were activated.

Wandering away from a silent and obtuse Cormac, Teddy headed toward the room connected to the great room and ducked inside, looking for an exit.

She made her way down the long hall and found she was right back in the kitchen, where there was a six-paned glass door. Peeking outside the window, she saw the door led to one of the entries to the hedge maze.

Popping it open and praying it didn't sound an alarm, Teddy slipped outside and turned her phone on, shivering as she waited for it to wake up.

She was calling this off. Right now. It was over. Screw the money. There had to be another way to get it.

As her phone lit up, she saw two things. The picture she'd sent her brothers of Cormac laying in the snow had never sent, which was likely a good thing—and there was a message in her voice mail inbox.

The piper was calling.

Oh shit.

Chapter 6

She clicked on the name and inhaled deeply before putting on her most professional tone and saying, "Theodora Gribanov here."

"You found him yet?" the voice at her ear, gruff and heavily laced with a Jersey accent, asked.

Fuck. Fuck. Fuckity-fuck. "It's been an entire thirty-two hours since you hired me. I told you these things can take time."

"Yeah, while you run up a fuckin' expense account on my dime, that kinda time? I damn well knew I shouldn't have hired a broad."

Moron. "Because there are so many places for a *broad* like me to shop in the forests of Colorado while I'm on a job. Speaking of, you can always fire me. In fact, I quit. Free of charge."

"Quit? What the fuck are you talkin' about? You just got started!"

Jesus, he was testy. What was the gig with this guy? "And now I'm damn well done, okay? So it's been real and all."

"What the hell is wrong with you?" he hissed in her ear. "I gave you a hefty pile of cash as a deposit to do a job, you bitch!"

Teddy clenched the phone in her hand, ready to lob it across the top of the hedge maze. "And I'll send your hefty pile of cash right back at'cha the second I get off this phone and I can transfer it from my account to yours. I'm out, hear me? Out. Later!"

She hung up while she still had the opportunity to cut him off and hit her bank account, transferring the lump deposit he'd made back to his account, and then she turned the phone off. She needed time with a computer to investigate this feeling in her gut that said something wasn't right. Whatever this was, she wanted no part of it anymore.

Teddy bit the inside of her cheek to keep from crying. She'd needed that money to help Sanctuary, and now it was gone with the wind. But no way was she getting into something that grew shadier by the second.

A tear slipped down her cheek for all the animals and wild birds that'd be farmed out to zoos and places they didn't belong, to be put on display because she'd never be able to get Sanctuary out of hock now. Mr. Noodles and Suits and Kim and Kanye would all suffer.

Then she swiped the tear away in anger. She was just tired. That was all. She'd figure out another way to do this.

Once she wasn't being hunted, that was.

Slipping back inside, she let her face rest against the cool wood of the doorframe, in the hopes she'd gather her thoughts before she had to face a crowd of people.

A hand thumped her back, clunky but gentle.

Lifting her head, she encountered Carl. A zombie. Or a half zombie. Or a zombie that looked nothing like the terrifying zombies on *The Walking Dead*.

Carl's sweet smile beamed down at her, childlike and open, if not a little green around the edges. He held up a plate of broccoli with a hand wrapped in duct tape.

Sucking in some air, she swallowed hard to keep from bursting into tears. "Oh, thank you, Carl. That's very sweet." Teddy took a stalk of broccoli and bit into it with a forced grin.

He bobbed his head. "Goo…d." He forced the word out.

Teddy smiled up at him, because you couldn't do anything but smile at Carl. "It's delicious. Did you cut this up yourself?"

Holding up his hand, she noted his finger was duct taped on and made a comical frowny face. "Assid...ent. Owwww," he moaned out, making her giggle.

Gripping his hand, Teddy pressed a kiss to his finger then held it to her cheek. "Aw, you cut yourself? I'm sorry, Carl. How about if tomorrow I show you how to chop vegetables so you never cut yourself again? I'm a really good cook."

His smile, if it was at all possible, grew wider. "Arrrrch, too?"

"Archibald? Aw, you bet, buddy. I could probably learn a thing or two from a master like him."

"Date." He pushed the word out from his lightly green-tinted lips before they turned upward in that ever-present smile.

"Best date ever," she returned.

Holding her hand, the zombie led her back through the kitchen and down the long hallway. Her eyes glanced at the majestic paintings of rocky cliffs and knights on horses mingled with neon bar signs on the wall as Carl dropped her right into the fray once again—to find everyone staring at her expectantly.

Teddy cleared her throat and made an attempt at keep her eyes direct. "Sorry...I got lost trying to find the bathroom. So where were we in Operation Keep Teddy in The Dark?"

Nina came around the corner, Lenny tucked under one arm, and threw a pillow at her, her almond-shaped eyes weary. "The part where you're grateful you have a place that's fucking safe to sleep. It's bedtime. I can't stay up like you crazy paranormals anymore. I need eight or you won't like the bitch you find in the morning over waffles and eggs over easy. So choose a room." She lifted Lenny's paw and pointed it at Teddy. "Tell the big bad bear it's night-night time for all Nosy Nellies."

Teddy looked upward at the huge spiral staircase of wrought iron and gleaming mahogany leading from the first floor, and frowned. "How many are there?"

"Twenty-two. How about I put you and your lumberjack right next to each other so you can sneak into each other's rooms? Make a right at the top of the stairs, third door on the left. Clean pajamas are on the dresser."

Cormac held out his arms to take Lenny from Nina, but she shook her head, rubbing her cheek on the cat's fluffy snow-white fur.

"Lenny can stay with me, where common sense and reason have sweet, unicorn-filled dreams. Isn't that right, Smooshie Face?" she asked the cat as he purred adoringly up at her.

Clearly, she wasn't going to find anything else out tonight, so she might as well get a good night under her before she found a way to break away from this group of women and figure this out.

She and Cormac bumped into each other as they each gripped the same knobby baluster with a bat carved into it on the staircase.

"Sorry," she murmured, her breathing erratic.

He backed away instantly and motioned for her to go ahead of him with a face carved of stone. As they made their way up the stairs, avoiding touching each other, her heart clenched in her chest. How could the two of them ever be life mates?

It was ridiculous to consider—especially under the tense circumstances.

And why had she blurted it out the way she had?

Because she'd been caught like a hooker in a jail cell and she'd panicked.

Not a good trait to possess in her line of side jobs.

What was done was done. And there was no hard and fast rule that said she had to mate with him. None that was enforced anyway. Maybe her feelings, this pull, this crazy attraction that had cropped up from the moment she'd looked into his eyes, was really something else.

Maybe it was adrenaline from the chase, or infatuation, and her heart, this thing pounding in her chest every time she looked at him, was just on overdrive. Because wouldn't a life mate reciprocate her chemistry? If Cormac was feeling anything, he gave good poker face.

Still, tomorrow was another day. Another day to find a way to explain to him why she'd shown up in the forest. Another day to attempt to figure out why someone wanted both she and Cormac dead.

"Night," she whispered before she pushed the door to her room open and left Cormac in the hall without looking back.

Upon entering, Teddy blinked. This couldn't possibly be a room in Nina Statleon's castle. It was pink—a millions shades of pink. Everywhere she looked it was pink, and ruffled, and so girlie-sweet, her teeth ached.

The queen-size bed featured a gauze and silk cotton-candy pink canopy cinched with a tiara at the ceiling that flowed over the sides of the bed, creating an almost cocoon of lush swirls. The quilted spread, complete with ruffles and yard after yard of silk fabric, fell to the plush pink carpeted floor.

Throw pillows in the shape of moons and stars in off-white were scattered over the surface and behind them, larger pillows covered in ruffled shams. A white rocking chair with a thickly padded seat sat by a window overlooking the hedge maze. Stacks of books sat to the left, everything from *Goodnight Moon* to *Cinderella* were piled high.

The walls were papered in white and pale-pink candy stripes with pictures of every Disney Princess ever and the arched windows with billowy pink curtains looked like they'd been stolen straight out of a fairytale.

A bathroom off to the left led to more pink and white tiles and a gorgeous porcelain pedestal sink in oyster with a shiny waterfall-like faucet at the center.

Teddy couldn't help but smile. This room was amazing—every girl's dream come true, and if she did nothing else, she intended to enjoy it until tomorrow, when she had to explain everything to Cormac.

Flipping the taps on the claw-foot tub, she gauged the water until it was nice and hot then dumped bubble bath, pink of course, by the boatload into the silky depths, smiling as the froth grew.

Stripping her dirty, bloody, torn shirt off, Teddy let it fall to the floor to inspect her wound in the mirror.

Almost all healed. The wound was nothing but a pink, puckered line along her side now, and by tomorrow it should be gone.

Kicking off her boots, socks and jeans, she grabbed some fluffy pink towels to drop beside the porcelain tub and slid in, groaning her pleasure at the instant ease her aches and pains were greeted with.

The aromatic scents of peonies and honeysuckle greeted her nose, making her close her eyes and inhale as she sank in up to her chin.

So Cormac. What did she know so far? Someone wanted him dead. He'd obviously been hiding out in the forest in Colorado for a reason. There was a person named Toni involved in all this somehow, and a guy named Andre had taken extreme measures to snuff him out.

And Cormac was delicious. Stoic, angry, sculpted, suspicious, maybe even a little resentful. But still delicious.

How did Nina, Marty and Wanda know Cormac? Was Toni the connection? She wished she had the gift of super-hearing like Marty and Wanda, but alas, bears were great trackers, scent being their biggest power, aside from sheer brawn. What had happened to his ring finger? Did that have to do with Andre, too?

Tomorrow, she'd have to find a way to call her brothers and explain—if that moron hadn't already done it by then.

Closing her eyes, she wondered about Andre. Andre sounded like a French name, but he hadn't spoken a word, so she didn't know for sure. Was Cormac a Russian bear like she and her brothers? Why did he look as though she'd asked him if he put his hair in curlers every night when she'd asked about his sleuth?

That was off, too. Everything was off, from her instincts to her judgment.

Yawning, she let her head fall back on the edge of the tub, stretching her calves and pointing her toes.

Exhaustion was seeping into her bones, meaning, she needed to wrap this up before she drowned and all the answers to her questions were left without resolution.

But it was so nice and warm, she was reluctant to leave. With a sigh, she sat up and grabbed the washcloth on the ledge of the window beside the tub and squeezed some of the luscious bath gel she'd found on the sink into it, lathering it up.

Just as she lifted her forearm to begin soaping up, a sharp crack and the silence of a suspended moment before the crash of glass made her eyes swivel to the window. Pieces of the window's heavy lead glass fell into the tub, sloshing bubbles and spraying water everywhere. A bullet skimmed her midsection before ricocheting off the picture on the wall opposite the bathtub.

Someone was shooting at her *now*? What the bloody fuck?

A million thoughts flew through her mind, but the foremost? Catch the son of a bitch who was taking potshots at her. Goddamn it, she was sick and effin' tired of being shot at. Anger, rife and raw, skittered up along her spine.

She didn't pay much attention to the screams of Wanda and Marty, or the commotion outside her beautiful bedroom door, or the pounding on the door by Cormac, all she saw was the color red.

She wanted the head of whoever was shooting at her on a pike.

In an instant, Teddy was in full shift. Her bones realigned with a satisfying crunch, the bulk of her torso spread, her haunches formed in a thick pair of solid muscles, her hair sprouted from every available pore and without thought, she launched herself out the window, sheetrock flying in every direction as she broke the wall surrounding the arched opening.

Dropping down to the first-floor roof, she lifted her nose, scented her target in seconds and hurled herself to the ground with a growl that would surely wake Nina's neighbors and have animal control on their way.

He was in a grand old oak tree, curled into a small ball in a corner where trunk met thick limb. He wore a bungee cord around his waist and climbing gear, likely how he'd managed to get up in the tree to begin with.

But there was no hiding from her—especially not in a tree. If there was anything Teddy Gribanov was skilled at, it was tree-climbing. Her brothers didn't even attempt to touch her record for hitting the top of a hundred-foot pine in thirty-four seconds flat.

Maybe it was because she was smaller, lighter than they were, but she beat them every time they challenged her.

Loping across the lawn at high speed, staying in the shadow of the hedge maze, the crunch of ice-covered grass beneath her feet, she headed straight for the tree, her eyes focused on the base.

She heard a gasp, which she was hoping like hell meant the guy taking shots at her was surprised by the fact that a bear had just shot out of a window and was running across the lawn. And then he confirmed his surprise when Teddy saw the gun fall to the ground, leaving a perfect outline in a cloud of freshly fallen snow.

There was no getting away from her, the shooter would have to repel down the tree and unhook his gear—she was too fast for him to accomplish that.

With a roar—an ugly, irate howl meant to inspire fear—Teddy launched herself at the base of the oak and shimmied upward, moving from branch to branch with the grace of a monkey.

Wanda, Nina, Marty and Cormac weren't far behind her, their arms waving as they raced across the lawn with Nina at the back of their pack, huffing and puffing.

But she couldn't hear their warnings she had the eye of the tiger and it was zeroed in on the bastard who, for whatever crazy reason, wanted her dead. Nothing mattered but getting her hands, er, paws on him.

The air was thick with his fear, his wide-eyed terror as she reached for him with a swipe of her paw, her claws poised to rip his throat open. She vaguely wondered how he'd gotten over the security gates surrounding Nina's vast property. But it didn't matter. He'd somehow gotten in, anchored a bungee around the tree, wrapped it around his waist and climbed up.

This was insane. Who wanted her dead this badly?

He stood on the limb then, his binoculars rolling to the back of his neck, the branches shaking in a tremble of ice and residual snow with his weight. The three-quarter moon shone on his face for a brief second, and that was her downfall.

Her complete shock. Her dismay.

What the hell was *he* doing here?

The shooter took that moment, that one faltered moment, to use the heel of his boot to knock her in the jaw, sending her crashing downward through branches that bashed against her back as she fell helplessly to the ground with another roar of frustrated anguish.

Teddy hit the top of the hedge maze, bouncing off and thudding to the ground with a crack of bones, knocking the wind out of her.

"Teddy!" Wanda screeched into the whistling wind. "Answer me!"

"Goddamn it, Nina, he's getting away!" she heard Marty yell.

"Got his gun!" Nina hollered back.

"Teddy! Where are you?" Cormac hollered, followed by heavy footsteps.

"Goddamn this hedge maze. I've lost more than one thing in this hot mess of foliage. Last time it was an earring, now it's a person. The next time I come through here, I'm doing it with a chainsaw, Vampire!" Marty bellowed.

"You leave my damn hedge maze alone, you animal!" Nina shot back. And then she yelled, "Kiddo! Answer us!"

"Do you think she's hurt?" Marty fret, her voice pitched much higher than normal.

"Nah. She fell from the top of a GD tree the size of King Kong, Marty. Don't talk crazy, moron," Nina groused back, breathing so heavily, Teddy heard the raspy gasps rattling across her eardrums.

"Shut up, Elvira Wannabe! You know what I mean!"

"Oh, blow me, Cupcake! How about you shut up—"

"Both of you shut up and help find Teddy!" Wanda wailed. "Teddy! Answer me, please!"

Teddy was too busy shifting back and attempting to catch her breath to muster the energy to yell, but she tried. "Over here!" she wheezed out. Damn it all, she'd definitely broken a rib on impact.

And she was naked.

Every lump and bump exposed when bright floodlights flashed on, turning the hedge maze into a football field.

And of course she was naked, because Cormac was the first to arrive on the scene, scaling a smaller hedge and dropping to his haunches upon landing.

He raced to her side, hunching down next to her, his eyes full of concern, keeping them on her face like any good gentleman would, running his hands over her cheeks. "Teddy, what the ever-lovin' hell?"

A cough rose up in her throat as the frigid air hit her exposed skin, making her hack and sneeze. Cormac pulled off his vest, wrapping it around her and pulling her close.

And she let him, naked as a blue jay, somehow comforted by this almost-stranger gathering her in his arms. She didn't understand it, he certainly wasn't Mr. Friendly, but he calmed the storm of anger at her missed opportunity to kill that son of a bitch.

Marty, Wanda, and finally a raggedly breathing Nina were there, too, fussing over her, throwing one of their bathrobes on her and helping Cormac get her up to her frozen feet and back into the house.

She grunted at the searing pain in her ribs, squeezing her middle like a vise, but she managed to hobble into the kitchen, where Nina took her from Wanda and Marty. Wrapping her arm around Teddy's waist, she brought her to a window seat, where a pile of plush cushions in cheerful red and navy blue were stacked.

"Sit. Stay. I'll make something to warm your *Braveheart* ass up."

Cormac was at her side before she could protest, gripping her frozen hands, warming them between his bigger ones. "Are you hurt? What happened? I heard some glass shatter and the next thing I know, you're hell on wheels across the lawn in bear shift."

Attempting a deep breath, Teddy shivered from her head to her toes. "Somebody took a shot at me. If you go upstairs to the bathroom, you'll find a bullet on the floor and a broken window over the bathtub, among other things."

"The motherfucker!" Nina griped, slamming a pot on her chef-sized stove. "He broke the window? Jesus, those windows with the fancy arch in them cost a damn fortune. I had that room specially decorated for my sister Penny because she loves fairy princesses. I'll kill the fuck!"

Marty, her hair a wild nest of curls, her silky lavender pajamas clinging to her, rolled her eyes. "Settle down over there, Threat-Maker. You're not killing anyone. I'll have Keegen send someone to fix it tomorrow. Penny will never know it happened." Then her blue eyes turned to Teddy as she brushed a strand of hair from her face with motherly fingers. "Are you okay, honey? Did he hit you? Let me look."

Wanda rolled up the sleeves of her long, flowing nightgown in sky blue and huffed a breath, her face wreathed in a sympathetic smile. "Oh, Teddy, you were magnificent! You climbed that tree like some kind of otherwordly creature. I've never seen something so big move so fast."

Teddy chuckled then grimaced at the pressure it put on her rib. "I've been doing it a long time. And I'm okay. I'll heal," she said for the second time in less than twenty-four hours. "How did he get in here anyway? I thought this place was locked up tight with all this high-tech security?"

"An apparent malfunction with the security gates. He got lucky because the gate is electric. Had it been working, he'd have fried to a crisp. But it'll be fixed in no time," Wanda assured.

Nina, in footy pajamas with red and white stripes, set a steaming cup down in front of her on the small table by the window seat and held up the gun she'd found by the tree. "You're one determined broad, huh? You were across that lawn lickety-split. You get a look at him? Was it that Andre dude again? How the fuck could he have gotten here so quick?"

Oh, she'd gotten a look at him, just before he'd knocked her fifty feet to the ground. But she couldn't tell them that. "I'm not sure, but I *am* sure it wasn't Andre. I don't get it."

Cormac ran a hand over his jaw, his beard rustling under his fingers. "I don't know what the hell's going on at this point. Maybe they thought I was in the room?"

Teddy shook her head, allowing Archibald, who'd rushed into the kitchen on silent feet, to press a heating pad against her ribs. "*No*. He had binoculars. That was meant for me. He must have been looking into Penny's window and found me. I feel it in my gut."

She knew beyond a shadow of a doubt he'd meant to kill her. How she'd explain that would have to wait until she investigated further. She'd only cause more grief and confusion without the facts.

Nina whistled as she settled in a chair at the round table, tucking her feet under her. "Okay, so now we have two fucks hunting you two? Shit just got real. What are we gonna do about it?"

"I agree with Nina. I know that's rare, but what *do* we do about it?" Marty asked, gripping a mug of her own.

"We get a good night's sleep and then we figure out who the players in this game are and hatch a plan," Wanda responded without hesitation.

As their voices became distant background noise, as Cormac held her hands and chatted with them, Teddy knew what she had to do.

She had to figure out why the guy who had hired her was trying to kill her.

Dakota Cassidy | Bearly Accidental

Chapter 7

She woke in the basement with a sick feeling of dread in the pit of her stomach for what this morning brought.

Today, she had to confess to the girls and Cormac about why she'd really darted him back in Colorado. No way he was going to believe her life mate claim after that. He'd think she made it up to save her own hide, but while that was partially true, it wasn't a total lie.

He *was* her life mate. He was meant to be hers, and now, even though he'd hate her guts once she confessed, she was going to make sure no one hurt him. Whether he liked it or not.

Rolling to her side, she hugged the pillow and moaned into it to keep from waking Cormac, who slept soundly on a twin bed not far from hers.

Nina had put them down here in the playroom her daughter Charlie and her cousins played in because there were no windows where people could turn her into a cadaver. It was a room built virtually underground, full of all sorts of toys and Barbie motorized cars—and unicorns. So many stuffed unicorns.

Sitting up, she pushed the warm blanket from her body and reached for the bathrobe Nina had loaned her, snuggling into it as she watched Cormac's wide chest rise and fall.

His arm was thrown over his forehead, his rippled-with-muscle chest exposed, the delicious trail of hair from his belly button snaking down under the sheet, dark and crisp-looking. Teddy wanted to run her fingers through it, burrow against his side, wrap her leg around his and nestle. He was a thing of beauty—every last inch of his hard body made hers tighten in curiosity, made her fingers itch to explore.

She had to take a deep breath when she simply looked at him. He was so beautifully rough; she had to force herself to continue taking air into her lungs.

"Are you watching me sleep?" he grumbled, deep and sleepy.

She jumped, her cheeks going red, her eyes shooting to the floor. "That's creepy. Why would I do that?"

He laughed that rumble of a laugh that made goose bumps appear on her arms. "This from the woman who darted me and hauled me over her shoulder like some cavewoman with a side of beef? You have some questionable moments, lady."

Teddy giggled and stretched. "How'd you sleep?"

"You mean when I wasn't worried to death about you?"

Her heart skipped a beat then settled in her chest. "You don't need to worry about me. Clearly, I can take care of myself."

"Yeah. Your broken rib and torn-up gut say so."

"I was trying to keep you from being shot, thank you very much."

"No," he murmured in a softer tone. "Thank *you* very much. You did save me from being shot. I've been a bit of an asshole about it ever since, haven't I?"

Teddy snorted, trying to smooth her bed-head into place without appearing obvious. "A bit? Define your means of measurement."

"Okay, a lot of an asshole. I apologize."

"How magnanimous," she replied, but she smiled when she said as much.

"How's the rib this morning?"

Her hand went self-consciously to just under her breast, where she pressed with two fingers. "Fine. Like it never happened."

"This healing thing is pretty amazing, huh?"

Teddy cocked her head. "You say that like you've just discovered it. You should have always been able to self-heal. From birth, in fact."

"Welp, I wasn't born this way. So seeing it happen and having confirmation I'm not crazy is all new to me."

"Come again?"

"I said I wasn't born this way—the way I assume you were. I was bitten."

Her hand flew to her mouth to cover her gasp. "*What?* Someone bit you? That's against our code!"

"There's a code?"

"Yes! A very strict one. If you break it, you're subject to some serious shit. We don't go around biting people just to bite them. It's 2016, for hell's sake."

"So you *used* to bite people to just bite them?"

"No. I mean, sure, we had rogues who did whatever the hell they wanted, but there weren't any penalties until the late seventies. Now if you bite someone and turn them, unless it's in self-defense, you end up in the pokey. We have rules, just like humans."

Cormac cleared his throat and propped himself up on the pillows, his thick chestnut hair against the white sheets falling to his jaw line in a sexy tousle. "Good to know. I don't need to end up in bear jail. I have enough trouble as it is."

Her head reeled so hard from this revelation, she was almost dizzy. Who would do such a thing? "*Who* bit you?"

"Andre."

Now her eyes almost fell out of her head as she hopped up and paced to his bed to look him in the eyes. How had she not smelled Andre was a bear? Had she been too pumped up on adrenaline? Too focused on saving Cormac that she'd missed a crucial clue?

He patted the bed and she didn't think twice about plunking down next to him, still in disbelief. "*What?* Andre bit you? How? When?"

Cormac's let out a puff of air from his luscious lips. "If he is indeed the same guy who you saw on my computer screen, then it was Andre. This is part of that long story I mentioned. The short of it is, we were in an accident together. A car accident. I was trying to get away from Andre in the rubble of the wrecked car and he bit my calf. I still have the scar, which, incidentally, didn't go away once I'd healed. How does *that* work with this self-healing method anyway?"

She almost didn't know what to say. She didn't know anyone who'd been turned into a bear—not ever. Everyone she knew, all her family, her friends, were all born bear shifters. "I don't know. Maybe it's because you weren't born this way? Because you were, in essence, manufactured?"

"I feel like a Lady GaGa song."

Teddy couldn't help but laugh but then she sobered. "So how did you get into a car accident with Andre and why was he trying to keep you from getting away?"

"Andre and his Russian mob-leader wannabe, Stas, kidnapped me when they found out my sister Toni shared some sensitive information about them with me."

On a wince, Teddy asked, "Sensitive how?"

"Murder."

"They murdered someone?" Things were becoming clearer by the second.

"My sister saw it. She managed to get away and she came straight to me. Unfortunately, they caught up with her at my house. Next thing I remember, they have me in some cellar in some house, threatening to hack off my finger if I don't tell them where Toni is. Somehow, she managed to escape them."

His voice held pride at this revelation, pride and love.

Teddy's eyes went to his missing ring finger, and *her* fingers moved of their own volition, grabbing his hand. "That's what happened to your finger. They cut it off…" She swallowed hard, her stomach rolling at what he and Toni must have endured. How horrific.

But at least she knew her gut had been right about Cormac. Thank God she still had an instinct working properly.

Cormac nodded his sleep-mussed head. "They used it as bait to prove to her they had me. They mailed it to her. Then they made a phone call, which is still sort of vague for me, because I was in and out of consciousness. But I assumed it was a call made to Toni, demanding a meet. I get the impression they told her they'd let me live if she'd meet with them. It's still a blur. I hadn't eaten in days. Hardly slept. I think by that point, I was delusional. I only know I got it in my head that it was her on the other end of that line and no way was I going to let them near her."

"Oh, Cormac…" she whispered, reaching out to cup his bearded jaw, the crisp hair tickling her palm. "How horrible. I don't know what to say."

His fingers curled around hers and he squeezed, brushing them to his lips. "I knew damn well they weren't going to let me go, but I was sick with worry she'd actually meet with them. I spent that whole damn ride racking my brain for a way to escape. But fate stepped in. We were, I think, on our way to meet her when we were T-boned. Somehow—and I have no idea how, other than the sheer will to survive—I managed to escape."

"And you've been hiding from them ever since," she offered in a somber whisper.

"Trying to figure out where my sister went—or if she was even alive—and who they'd murdered that night. I needed some kind of proof to go to the authorities with. I watched the news for days after the murder. It happened at a pretty high-profile car dealership. That was where Toni worked. But there was nothing. Not a single word. No body means no murder."

"So Toni didn't know the dead guy?"

"No. Not according to her. I'll never forget her face when she showed up at my door that night, white as a ghost, shaking so hard I didn't know if I'd ever calm her down, and verging on hysteria. She'd found out Stas, her boyfriend at the time, was cooking the books at the dealership. She'd called her supervisor, Andre—"

"Andre was her supervisor?" Oh, Jesus.

"Yep. Anyway, she called him with the proof, and he asked her to meet him to straighten things out. When she showed up for that meeting, Stas and Andre were standing around, laughing about the poor soul they'd just murdered. And that's all I know."

A shiver of fear rolled over her spine. "Where is Toni now?"

He grinned, warm and fond, making him a million times more appealing than he was before, if that was even possible. "She's okay. That's where Nina, Marty, and Wanda come in. They met Toni at a discount designer mall in Jersey where she was working. It gets crazier from there—I'm not sure you're up for it."

"Crazier than you being bitten by a Russian mob guy and turned into a bear? Please. Go on and try me," she teased.

He looked hesitant until she nudged his hip with her knee. "Toni fell through a wormhole at the designer outlet store she was working in and where the three women and Carl were shopping for Christmas. They fell into another realm called Shamalot, where she met the love of her life and plans to marry. One Prince Iver of Castle Beckett, I believe."

Teddy rolled her tongue against the inside of her cheek and blinked. "Okay, you're definitely testing the parameters of crazy. How do you know this for sure? I don't want to doubt the Bickersons, but you have to see how outrageous this sounds, don't you?"

Cormac's laughter echoed around the basement. "I do see how outrageous it sounds, but Wanda had a message from my sister—one that could have only come from her or my best friend Damon. Oh, and a tattoo parlor in Atlantic City."

"Care to divulge this information?"

"Uh, nope," he said on a delicious grin.

"Okay, fine. So you trust they're telling you the truth?"

"I do. Can't say why, other than it's not like I don't understand an outrageous story. How many people would believe me if I told them I was turned into a bear by an angry Russian mobster? Besides, what do they have to benefit in pretending to help me?"

"Maybe lead you right to the Russian mob dude who wants to kill you?"

"Because?"

Suddenly, she was getting a much clearer picture of the attempt on her life last night. "Okay, for the sake of our predicament, let's say what they're telling you is true. What can they do to fix this problem?"

"I don't know, but according to them, they're pretty proficient at this kind of thing. Did they tell you about OOPS?"

Teddy's head bounced up and down. "The support for paranormals in crisis? Yes. I heard all about it from Nina. Apparently, she was once the bruiser of this bunch."

As they'd all settled into the castle last night, Nina had shown her the OOPS website and told her all about how each of them were turned. She'd only listened with half an ear, too caught up in her own fears to totally focus, but she vividly remembered something about genies and cougars and dragons. Oh yes. She remembered the bit about the dragons.

"She gave up her vampirism for Toni. She saved her life from an evil queen."

Teddy snorted a laugh, unable to keep it from shooting from her mouth.

Cormac laughed, too. "I know. I know, but what choice do I have but to believe!"

"Right. Okay, now you've gone too far, buddy. An evil queen? Seriously?"

"Um, yeah. Seriously," Nina said, suddenly standing before them, crumbs at the corner of her mouth from the cinnamon Pop Tart she held, Lenny tucked securely under her arm. "You got some kinda problem with that?"

God. She was like a cat.

Cormac and Teddy passed each other guilty glances. "You have to admit, it's pretty outlandish," she said with a sheepish glance up at the tight-faced ex-vampire.

Nina stuffed a hand inside her black hoodie, shoving the Pop Tart in her pocket, and leered down at Teddy. "I don't gotta admit shit. You don't have to believe a fucking word that comes out of my mouth. I don't give a guinea pig's fart. What you best believe is this: people want you two dead. I get why they want Cormac dead, but I don't get why they want *you* dead, Teddy Bear. But I'm gonna find out. Now, quit loafin' around down here like you're on fucking vacay at Chez Statleon, waitin' on the breakfast bell while your towels warm in the dryer and someone steams your sheets. Get dressed and get your asses upstairs so we can figure it out. We have shit to do."

Teddy reached out a hand to Nina to apologize. "I'm sorry, Nina. I didn't mean to offend you. I was just…"

Nina frowned, her beautiful face scrunching up in disapproval as she set Lenny on Teddy's bed. "You were just flappin' those lips to flap. I get it. You're a chick. You say chick shit. But I lost my damn vampy powers for a reason, and it's not something you two insensitive shits straight outta Goldilocks have any business snarkin'. I stopped that lunatic bitch Angria from killing Toni because she's my GD friend, and the hell I was gonna let some whacked-out, jealous queen take her out. Toni was some badass in Shamalot. Always lookin' out for everyone but herself. You have no idea what she went through to get where she is. So don't make light about something you don't know a damn thing about. That shit happened, and your sister's one of the baddest bitches in the land. Don't ever make the ha-ha in front of me about it again."

This side of Nina, this protective, almost mother bear side, not only intrigued Teddy, it made her long to have a female influence in her life just like her.

Okay, maybe all the swearing and threats could be left out of that wish. But Nina was fierce about her loyalties and her friendships, and it was evident in her tone. What was also evident was her selflessness. She'd saved Toni, if the story was true. Who did that for someone they hardly knew?

Nina was clearly still touchy about losing her vampiric powers, but she made no bones about the fact that she'd done it out of allegiance and, by her definition, out of friendship.

"Nina, I had no idea," Cormac intervened, his voice gruff. "I mean, I knew you kept her from being killed, and you bit this Angria, and that by drinking her tainted blood you all surmise the act stole your powers, but I didn't know how close you'd become to my sister. I'm sorry. I meant no disrespect for what you did for Toni. I'll never forget that kind of loyalty. If there's anything I can ever do, you just have to say the word."

Nina tucked her hair behind her ears, her eyes narrowed. "Well, you might know if you didn't spend all your time brooding in the corner. Your sister tried like hell to find you, pal—from the day those dick-knuckles took you. She loves you, and the guilt she felt over thinking she'd lost you was big, brother. Bigger than she is. She hated that she hid away in Jersey all that time. She was all torn up with guilt that she didn't know what happened to you. That maybe there was something else she could have done to find your ass. Toni figured if she was alive, she could at least bring to justice the fuck that did you in, and she tried hard. Which was a fucking smart move. So here's the score, Moody Blues, she can't ever come back here if you don't get off your butt and play an active part in taking these assholes out. So get the fuck up, Pooh Bear. No more mopin'. We have a Russian mob boss to bag."

Nina turned on her heel, stalking off toward the entry to the basement and back upstairs, the slamming of the door the only sound.

Teddy puffed her cheeks out, intending to rise and get a move on. Even without powers, Nina was pretty scary. She shuddered thinking of the damage she must have caused *with* them.

Cormac grabbed her hand and voiced that very thought. "Imagine her with the strength of ten men."

Teddy's head fell back on her shoulders as she tried to stifle a giggle while Lenny settled next to her. "And fangs."

Cormac laughed.

"I fucking hear you!" Nina yelled after popping the door open. "Imagine me coming down there and beating your face with your own leg after I chew it clear off. Get the fuck up here or I'm sending Wanda the Warden in!"

Both Teddy and Cormac looked at each other in panic. "No," she whispered, mocking horror. "Not Wanda!"

Cormac's chest rose and fell, barking more laughter as he slid from the bed and reached for his jeans.

That was exactly when more guilt set in. First, because she had to tear her eyes away from him. Second, because the guillotine was poised over her head, just waiting to hack it off. She couldn't keep hiding her reasons for being here, and after Cormac had confessed what this Andre wanted from him, how could she keep something as vital as the information she had to herself? The time to come clean was here.

The news she was about to share made her grateful Nina was no longer a vampire.

She was pretty okay with her face, and she was sort of fond of her legs remaining attached.

Chapter 8

After a shower, wherein she stalled for as long as possible, she made her way back upstairs, where Carl greeted her with a hot cup of coffee and pointed to the kitchen table where everyone had gathered.

Heaps of food were piled high on plates, fluffy yellow scrambled eggs, bacon, sausages and croissants were in abundance, while Archibald, dressed as immaculately as last night, like some food maestro, orchestrated the meal. His joy at having everyone together was obvious in his twinkling eyes and spry step.

Teddy's stomach growled in appreciation.

Until she remembered what she had to do.

Tell the truth.

As she looked for an open seat, Cormac smiled and patted the one next to him. The day was gray and snowy just outside the sprawl of big windows enveloping the breakfast nook, where Lenny napped on a pillow Nina had Archibald bring him, but it didn't dull his gruff good looks.

His warm, inviting smile did things to her stomach, and her heart, somehow syncing up, creating a riot of unsettled emotions.

As she sat next to Cormac, he leaned into her and whispered in her ear, "You feel better?"

"Is Nina still going to eat my legs off?"

He chuckled, sending a ripple of awareness along her arms. "Nah. Well, maybe only one leg."

Teddy shuddered, tucking her down vest around her. "Scary ex-vampire is scary."

"So scary."

"What are you two making googly eyes over now? Eat some damn food. You're gonna need all your brain cells today, Teddy Bear. Nothin' better to start the hunt for Russian motherfluffers than a good breakfast." Nina shoved the plate of eggs at her, popping a piece of bacon in her own mouth as she did.

The heavy weight of her confession, one she'd practiced over and over in her head, began to blur and swim in her brain. Taking the eggs, she put some on her plate, listlessly poking at them with her fork.

"Hey, you'd better call your brothers huh?" Marty suggested, batting her eyelashes. "They're probably wondering why you didn't bring your life mate home."

As pretty as the day before, Marty had let her hair down this morning. It fell in beachy waves around her beautiful face, artfully made up to enhance the deep blue of her eyes. She wore a cute pair of denim leggings and knee-high boots with a thigh-length cable-knit sweater in purple.

Looking down at her freshly laundered torn clothes, Teddy suddenly found herself feeling quite small. When she'd reached the age where clothes and makeup became important to her, her mother was already gone.

Her brothers had raised her from that point on, and they knew zero about clothes and all things girl, especially as young as they'd been when they'd taken the reins from their mother. They knew horses and running a ranch and a business. They'd done their best to give her everything she needed, and she loved and appreciated them more than they'd ever know, but sometimes...

Sometimes, she wished for a female influence—someone to tell her what color sweater made her eyes stand out or how she should wear her hair.

Instead, she pulled her own wavy hair up in a ponytail or braided it—because it was practical when working with the animals she loved so much.

"Teddy, honey?" Wanda leaned over the table and patted her arm. "Your brothers? Shouldn't you call them?"

The last thing she wanted to do was call Vadim and Viktor with the kind of news she would impart. She'd lost a lot of cash…

She shrugged and swallowed. "I wasn't sure if you'd be okay with it. But I guess I should, if you all don't mind."

Wanda tugged the end of Teddy's braid and smiled. Just as perfectly made up as Marty, she was also equally as beautiful. "I'm sorry. I was pretty grumpy yesterday, wasn't I?"

Hah. Just you wait, Wanda.

Teddy shrugged again, almost afraid to say anything. "It was a tense situation. I understand."

But Wanda shook her head, smoothing back her updo with elegant fingers and a grin. "I was a bear, if you'll pardon the pun. But I'd been listening to Marty and Nina argue with each other for four days while we tried to figure out Cormac's exact location. Our directions were pretty vague. As you can imagine, the twins had drained me of my energy by the time we found him."

Wanda was their peacemaker—that was as clear as the day was long. She was the leader of the pack whether she acknowledged it or not, this pack they'd created out of necessity, and the burden of keeping Marty and Nina from killing each other had to be on par with wrestling alligators every single day.

"I take it it's been hard on you with this change for Nina?"

Wanda sighed as she sipped her coffee, the gesture forlorn. "It's been hard for all of us, but Marty's taking it the hardest. Maybe even harder than Nina. Nina seems to be just fine as long as she has food. But fear not, we'll figure it out. In the meantime, go call your brothers and let them know you're safe. I'll feel better and so will you." Patting her arm once more,

Wanda turned back to the conversation Nina and Cormac were having about the Giants and the Steelers.

Giving her permission to call her brothers was like giving her permission to attend her own funeral.

Pushing the spindled chair out, Teddy reluctantly rose and made her way back to the great room where it was quiet.

She took a seat on the very couch she'd sat on last night, by the fire where it was warm, and pulled her phone from her pocket, turning it on.

There were tons of texts from both Vadim and Viktor. They began pretty lighthearted. "*Hey, you okay?*" and "*Little sister, where you at?*"

But they began to go sour after the first four or five. "*You're freaking us out, Teddy Bear!*" and "*If you don't check in soon, we're comin' for you!*"

The worst was, "*Don't do this shit to us, Teds! Not after last year. Get in touch now!*"

She typically kept in pretty close contact with them whenever she was on a job. The total silence had them in a panic, and with good reason, after what had happened last year. Yet, she had no choice but to relieve their worries.

Oddly, there was no text about the job itself or the events that had unfolded last night. Probably because her treetop hit man didn't want anyone to know what he'd done to the person he'd hired.

Finding Vadim's number, she clicked on it and winced. Here went nothin'.

"Jesus Christ, Teddy, it's been more than twenty-four hours! Are you okay? Do you need us? Where the hell are you and where's Cormac Vitali?" Vadim shouted, his voice rife with panic and fear.

Blowing out a breath of pent-up air, she said, "I'm fine, Vadim. Relax. Everything is fine."

"I'm putting you on speaker so Viktor can stop wearing a hole in the damn floor. Jesus and hell, Teddy! You scared the shit out of us!"

"Teddy?" her brother Viktor roared, curling her eardrums. "What in blazes is going on? Do you have any idea how worried we were? When I say call and keep in touch during a bounty, I mean call and keep in touch!"

She pictured Viktor and Vadim, pacing the worn length of the hardwood kitchen floor in their ranch house, running their hands over the light brown scruff on their faces, in tune with one another's every move.

"Okay, okay! Wait, please! Just let me explain. Everybody calm down and let me talk. No interruptions. Agreed?"

"It better be good, Theodora," Vadim hissed.

Most people couldn't tell her identical brothers apart, but she didn't have any trouble at all because their differences were distinct. Vadim was the less high-strung of the two; his swagger was more relaxed, his face less scrunched up in a frown, his overall vibe down to earth.

Viktor, on the other hand, was always wired for sound. Ready to go at a moment's notice, all pent-up energy and motion. Both worried about her in equal measure, they just did so very differently, and right now, she wasn't up to the interrogation.

Tucking her legs under her, Teddy sighed. "First, Cormac Vitali isn't the bad guy here. Now, hold on…" She heard Viktor's simmer, even over the phone. "Don't start yelling about sympathizing or whatever psychobabble you two keep coming up with until I explain. And if you're not going to stay calm while I do it, I'm hanging up."

Vadim huffed into the speaker. "But that's exactly what I'm going to do. What have we told you about sympathizing with the bounty, Teddy? Stop trying to figure everyone out and fix their damn boo-boos and just bring 'em in. That's the job we gave you."

"You're not listening. I'm not sympathizing with the bounty. I'm telling you, Cormac Vitali isn't the bad guy. That bastard of a client is! The one who hired us with his pathetic story about catching the guy who killed his friend! Know how I know? I'll tell you how I know, brothers. That client tried to kill me last night. *Kill me.*"

She still had trouble believing it, but it was true. The man who'd been taking potshots at her last night was the very man who'd hired her to bring in Cormac Vitali.

There was a silent moment while Teddy allowed them to absorb her words. She'd stunned them speechless. That almost made her giggle. Except, that client had paid them a lot of money as a deposit to find Cormac, and they'd just *lost* a lot of money because he was dirty.

They had a mortgage to pay and a ranch to run. She'd have to find a way to make it up to them somehow.

"So you're telling me, the client from Jersey, Arty McDaniels—"

"Probably not his real name," she interjected.

"Okay, the guy with the potentially fake name who was carrying on about how Cormac had killed his friend, the friend he wanted justice for, was the same guy who tried to kill you last night?" The disbelief in her brother's voice rang in her ear clear as a bell.

"That's exactly what I'm telling you. Same guy climbed a damn tree opposite the room I'm staying in and took a shot at me just last night. I went after him and I saw him, Vadim. Saw him with my own two eyes. He got away, but it was the same damn guy."

She was still parsing it in her mind, trying to make sense of all this. McDaniels told all three of them the sob story of his dead friend with real tears glistening in his eyes as he'd hired them. He'd told them all about how he was determined Cormac be brought to justice in honor of his alleged dead friend. All he wanted was for them to locate the mark and bring him in, where he'd gladly help her bring Cormac to the nearest police station.

That was when Viktor and Vadim had stopped him cold. They never asked for the emotional details surrounding a bounty—it was too personal. All they needed was the cash and the assurance that, once the bounty was found, the client agreed to let them aide in escorting the bounty to the police department. It was unconventional, yes. But their reasons for taking bounties to begin with were very personal.

But that wasn't what Arty McDaniels had wanted at all—she knew it in her gut. He'd wanted Cormac found all right, he wanted him found so he could kill him, and she'd helped him find the man he wanted to murder.

The more she thought about it, the more she was sure she had a much better picture of what had likely really happened the night McDaniels' "friend" was allegedly murdered, and it had nothing to do with Cormac.

He was damn well in cahoots with these Russians somehow. They needed to shut Cormac up before he found the right cop to listen to him—unlike the cops his sister had tried to convince.

"So all that bullshit about bringing Cormac to justice in honor of his buddy was crap? How the hell did he get this Vitali into the system to begin with? Did he hack it?"

Arty McDaniels had come complete with loads of information from official sites, all declaring Cormac was wanted for the murder. "I guess if he was willing to come to us for help in capturing Cormac with a fake name and a fake story, he'd surely be prepared to create falsified documents. And why else would he try to kill me if his story wasn't bullshit? Why would he want me dead if I found Cormac for him? Did he get suspicious because I'd come to New York?"

"New York? What the hell are you doing in New York?" Viktor yelped.

Squeezing her temples, Teddy clenched her teeth. "It's a long story, and I'll explain in a minute. But what I'm sure of is, McDaniels wants anyone who came in contact with Cormac and might've heard the real story dead. He just needed him found. Was the plan always to kill us *both* after I'd found him, and make us disappear just like his buddy? No one would know the truth, right? You'd both think I got lost on the bounty. The forest is a big place, Viktor, but he needed someone who knows it like we do—like *I* do. Also, no one's looking for Cormac but his sister, and she's at the root of all this. She's the one who saw what happened. So who'd know the difference?"

"What *is* the real story, Teddy? What happened with this guy's sister and why the hell are you in New York?" Vadim asked.

As she explained what Cormac had told her this morning about Stas and Toni and why she'd come to New York, leaving out the part about Shamalot and life mates, her brothers listened in silence.

When she was finished, Viktor finally spoke. "That means this was all some kind of crazy setup. He just needed someone skilled to track Vitali. I'll hunt his sorry ass down, Teddy. He'll beg for death when I'm done with him!" he bellowed into the phone, followed by the slam of a fist. Probably on the center island, if the sound of plastic apples falling to the ground was any indication.

Then another wave of horror hit her. "You know what else this means, don't you? If he came for me, he might come for you guys. He won't want anyone left to identify him. You and Vadim aren't safe."

"Screw safe. I dare the jackass to come at me."

"Viktor, save the Superman bit," she scolded. "I'm just asking that you watch your backs. Please. At least until I figure this out. And maybe do a little investigating with some of your contacts. Find out who this Arty McDaniels really is."

Viktor lowered his voice then, gentling his tone. "You don't owe this Vitali anything, you know. How were you supposed to know our client was a maniac?"

Except, she did owe Cormac something. She'd helped this McDaniels find him. Handed him over on a silver platter. But it wasn't just that. He was her intended. She'd avoid telling her brothers that for now, but she knew. She just needed to get used to the idea before she shared it with more people than those who already knew.

"I do owe him something, Viktor. I led McDaniels straight to him, and while I didn't know that then, I know it now. What have we always said about this bounty business? Sure, it makes us money, but we find bad guys law enforcement can't because we can track better than any human ever could. We do it because of what happened to Dad. In his honor."

There was a low grumble from Vadim at the mention of her father, but it was a clear reminder of their reasons for taking up bounty hunting to begin with. It had begun to avenge his murder when no one else would investigate deeper. It had ended with Vadim near death, but they'd caught the bastard, and they continued to catch bastards for that very reason.

Some people managed to escape the law. Teddy and her brothers ensured criminals were brought to justice. They only took cases where the client agreed to meet with law enforcement officials if the bounty was captured—which McDaniels had agreed to do. In fact, he'd signed a contract saying as much.

They'd had all sorts of bounties over the years, deadbeat dads, murderers, domestic abuse cases, escaped convicts, and they never varied from their mission in honor of Maxim Gribanov. Put the bad guys away for good; truth, justice, the American way—or some such noble cause.

"But do you remember the last time you got this involved, Teddy? Look, I only say this because we almost lost you. That you're even out on this bounty now was enough to send both of us over the edge. We didn't like it. We'd have done it for you and given you the money if not for all that pride you have when it comes to being independent. I know you need the money for Sanctuary, but it isn't worth your life."

The animals at Sanctuary *were* her life, but no one understood that in quite the way another activist passionate about preserving wildlife would. "I remember what happened, and I promise you, this isn't like that. Swear it on my trusty dart gun," she joked.

"So why not just take this to the law there in New York, Teddy?"

 "And say what? This random guy who probably gave us a fake name hired us for a bounty he never intended to pay up on because really, all he needed was someone who knew the forest to track down the guy he wanted to murder himself? Besides, did you listen to what I told you about the police and Cormac's sister? What if the one guy we turn to is dirty like in Toni's case? This is the mob we're talking about, Vadim. They hacked off Cormac's finger, for Christ's sake."

The idea made her want to spit nails. Toni had done the right thing, only to end up losing three years of her life in hiding because the cops were on the take. Who did you trust? No way was she taking a chance on trusting the wrong person.

"Okay, so we come to you and bring you home and keep you safe until we figure this out. End of," Viktor said.

"No!" she shouted into the phone. "I'm not leaving." Crap. How was she going to explain wanting to stick this out to them? She'd have to tell them the truth, and then they'd claim her judgment was clouded by lust.

"Why the hell not?" Vadim yelped.

"Because I'm not. I started this. I virtually handed Cormac's location over to McDaniels. I'm not just going to run away from my part in this. Is that what you two taught me to do? Run away from my responsibility?"

Vasim blustered with a huff. "Don't you think this is a little different than when you helped Kevin Lightfoot steal his brother's X-Box 360 by hoisting him up onto the trellis so he could sneak into his brother's room? It's *way* different, Teddy. We're talking a guy is trying to kill you. *Kill* you."

She got his point. She'd definitely helped Kevin Lightfoot steal his brother's X-Box 360. She'd gone into it with the promise she could play *Halo*. Okay, so she didn't directly steal it, but her brothers had made her own up to her part in the whole mess because she was guilty by association.

"You're right; it's not the same thing exactly. But I'm not leaving. And I already told you, I have a werewolf and a hybrid and a very ragey ex-vampire watching my back. I'm safe with them. Promise."

Vadim barked at her, "How do you know you can trust these people? You don't even know them. That's insane."

"I don't know anything. I just know I'm an adult. Cormac's been on the run for three years. We were going to collect a hefty bounty if we caught him, and even after I sent that jackhole his money back, I ended up leading that prick McDaniels right to him and he tried to kill me. Because he now knows that *I* know he was full of shit, telling us Cormac killed his friend. No way I'm walking away from this. Look, I have to go. I love you both. I promise I'll keep in closer touch. I have a confession to make to Cormac and the ladies. In the meantime, why don't you two go drum up some business now that we've lost the Vitali bounty and it'll be on me—"

"Teddy! This isn't about the damn money!" Viktor shouted.

But she knew better than to try to convince them she was doing the right thing. "Stop yelling at me and listen. I'm going to trash this phone because it wouldn't surprise me if McDaniels tapped it to track me. He managed to find out I was here in New York somehow. I'll get the burner from my backpack and text you with the number. Talk to you soon. I love you both."

She hung up to their loud protests and closed her eyes, blowing out a long breath.

Okay, so one confession down, one more to go. The worst of it was yet to come, but she was determined to get everything out in the open.

"The Vitali bounty?"

Fuck all.

Chapter 9

Cormac's voice, full of anger, forced her to acknowledge his presence whether she wanted to or not. Flames crept up along the back of her neck and onto her cheeks. Licking her lips, Teddy gazed up at him. Gone were the soft glances he'd shot her way over breakfast, now replaced with hot eyes full of accusation.

Closing her eyes again, she inhaled and said, "I know what this sounds like, Cormac, but I need you to just hear me out. Please. This wasn't how I meant for you to find out."

"Aw, c'mon, *Teddy Bear*. You didn't mean for me to find out at all. Skip the bullshit."

He'd had a hard enough time trusting Wanda and crew—to ask him to trust her once she told him why she'd really been out in the woods was going to be impossible. But she was going to give it a hella shot anyway.

"Just let me explain. Just hear me out. You can do whatever you want when I'm done."

That pulse in his jaw ticked; even beneath his beard she could see his fury. "Can't wait for this explanation. Are they going to be as lame as all the others? You know, like I'm your life mate? Gotta tell ya, I was this close to believing you. You're really good."

Jumping up from the couch, Teddy almost tripped over the four-foot tall silver knight in shining armor Nina had next to the fireplace, holding the poker. "That's not how it was, Cormac. I was telling you the truth when I said you were my life mate."

God, even to *her* ears that sounded shady.

Oh Lord. How was she ever going to explain this to him? How could she ever make this right, make him understand? She should have said something right from the get-go. The second she realized Cormac wasn't the bad guy and before they'd come to New York.

Her stomach pitched and rolled, but she forged ahead. "If you'll just hear me out. Let me tell you what's really going on; it might not make anything better, but at least you'll know the truth. I'll leave if you still want me to when I'm done."

The thought of leaving wrenched her gut, and this after just two days. It was almost unbelievable, except for the stories her mother had told her about how she'd know. How she'd doubt the validity of her feelings, how she'd have to be patient and allow them to grow, but Masha Gribanov had been firm on one thing—she'd know.

Nina's dark head popped around the corner just then, her expression irritated. "Dudes? What the fuck is the holdup in here? Are you two already playing kissy-face? Christ, it's been less than two days. Does anybody bother to get to know each other before they're skippin' off to play hide the salami? Jesus and some overactive hormones, you kids these days. You know too much. I blame social media," she said on a snort.

But no one was laughing.

Cormac began to speak, but Teddy held up her hand. "Nina? Would you ask everyone to come in here, please? I need to talk to you all."

Nina exhaled with a loud grunt. "We have shit to do, people. Do you know what day it is? It's fucking Sunday. *The Walking Dead's* on Sunday. It's Carl's favorite show. It's Nina and Carl time, every week on Sunday. We put Charlie to bed, we roast up some broccoli, and we watch his sorta people eat other people while Rick Grimes cries and I eyeball Daryl and his bow and arrow. I wanna wrap this shit up so I can get my Daryl on in peace without all the whiny, 'OMG, my life's in danger' shit hanging over my head. Also, Facebook never fails to fuck it up for me with spoilers. You'd think it took an act of God to put a spoiler alert in your post. But no, that jackhole friend of my husband's, Norman, is all up in my feed every GD time. What's so important that we're not gettin' on with this crap already?"

"I lied," Teddy blurted out, swallowing hard.

Nina's beautiful eyes narrowed, placing her hands on her slender hips. "About?"

"Pretty much everything," Cormac said.

"Not everything!" Teddy defended on a shout. Almost everything. There was a difference.

"I knew it!" Nina barked with a clap of her hands. "I fucking knew it. There's always something. Who says I need my special spidey powers to detect bullshit? Didn't I say that from the frickin' start? You got some secret, Teddy Bear, and it's gonna mess everything up. Then everyone's gonna be all in an uproar. Pooh Bear over here's gonna be all mopey and broody. You're gonna be all drippy snot and tears. Swear to God, I could've written down how this was gonna go. Fuck. Fuck. *Fuck!*"

"Nina!" Wanda tapped her friend on the shoulder, her stern teacher's face in full disapproval mode. "Why are you carrying on? Did we run out of Doritos already?"

Nina threw up her hands and rolled her eyes. "Because we got trouble. Just like we always do. Teddy says she has something to say. You know what that something is, Wanda? It's some confession that will keep these two knuckleheads from focusing on what's important. Catching that motherfucker Stas. It's just like it always is. Sure, the players are different. It's not a vampire or a genie this time but a damn pair of bears. And no, we didn't have to go through the whole, 'I can't believe I'm paranormal' bullshit therapy session we usually have to give our moron clients, but it's all the same in the end."

Wanda's gaze turned to them. Gone was the gentle, sympathetic Wanda, replaced by suspicious, tell-me-everything-or-I'll break-your-legs Wanda. "What's going on?"

"I'd like everyone here so I only have to say this once," Teddy said.

"Ass-sniffer? Stop curlin' your fake eyelashes and get the fuck in here!" Nina crowed toward the kitchen area.

Marty flew around the corner, her boots skidding to a halt when she slammed into Nina and almost dropped Lenny. "What's wrong?"

"Please sit, Marty," Teddy requested, keeping her eyes averted from Cormac's stony gaze.

As they all took their places on the couch—well, except for Cormac, who defiantly stood in the doorway—Teddy fought to keep tears from falling from her eyes.

She didn't even know these people, and now she was going to tell them something that would make them hate her guts.

Way to make friends, Teddy Bear.

* * *

"You're a fucking bounty hunter?" Nina asked, and if Teddy was correct, there was a hint of admiration in her tone. Which was better than her scorn. Nina's scorn hurt, and she didn't have a reason why, but it stung like a thousand bees.

However, she didn't want praise. She wanted them to give her the kind of hell she deserved for keeping this from them, and then she wanted forgiveness.

From a group of people she hardly knew. Why?

When she finally answered, her voice sounded small to her ears. "Not in the conventional sense, I guess. But that's mostly what we do. We're usually hired privately, and we always tell our clients they have to agree to meet with law enforcement if the bounty's caught. There are no exceptions, and we make them sign a contract to that effect. Then we hunt the bounty down and bring them in. We're really good trackers because we're bears. It gives us an advantage. Also, I know the forest like my own backyard. So when we have a bounty in Colorado, I almost always take it. Oh, and…on a final note, my last name isn't Jackson, it's Gribanov."

"So the dart gun story was a lie?" Marty inquired, crossing her arms over her chest.

She looked directly into Marty's eyes and nodded. "I'm sorry. I do use it for my work with the animals at Sanctuary, that's my day job, but as described by Arty McDaniels, we knew Cormac would be too big to contain without some help."

Nina beamed from her place on the couch and slapped her thigh. "Hah! You're a salty bitch, kiddo. I don't see what the fucking problem is. She did her job. Now she's telling us about it. What's the big shit in that?"

"Well, you wouldn't, ex-bloodsucker, because you're dead and cold inside. Your heart is black and shriveled," Marty reminded. "She told Cormac he was her life mate, Nina. You know how serious that is in our circles."

"Okay, let's be fair to Cormac. I did lie to him. He has a right to be angry," Teddy defended, and hoped she didn't sound like she was sucking up. "But I wasn't lying about his role in my life. It caught me off guard, too, but Cormac *is* my life mate."

She just had to wait until he knew it, too. Would he know? Ever? Her mother hadn't ever told her much about how her father had felt during their courtship. Had he known her mother was the woman for him?

When Cormac finally spoke, it was to condemn her. "Nah. I don't believe that. I'm just your cash cow."

Clenching her teeth, Teddy repeated, "I told you, I called the bounty off last night when I realized something wasn't right. I can't prove that to you, but it's the truth. I can prove the return of the money, if you're interested. I can show you my account at my bank." She paused and took a deep breath. "Look, you *should* be angry with me. That's only fair. But as angry as you are, we have a bigger problem. We have targets on our heads right now, Cormac. We don't have time to argue with each other about what a liar I am."

"But here's a question for you, *life mate*. Why should I believe this isn't some huge ruse? How do I know that 'attempt' on your life wasn't just some show you were putting on?"

Teddy glared at him hard, ignoring his dark beauty, ignoring his anger. "Because you woke up this morning. If I was a part of this, don't you suppose I would have just killed you in the forest? Or even if I didn't get a chance to do it then, why wouldn't I have whacked you in your sleep? You're not a stupid man, Cormac, but that was a stupid theory."

He glared back at her, but he kept his gorgeous mouth shut.

"So what you're telling us is the gentleman who hired you is the man who tried to kill you last night? You're sure?" Wanda asked, the wheels in her head clearly turning.

Teddy nodded. "I'm as sure as the nose on my face."

"Which grows longer by the second," Cormac snarked.

"Oh, shut the fuck up, Lumbersexual, and quit beatin' the kid down," Nina ordered, her brow furrowed in a deep frown. "Think about what it was like for your brooding ass to take a chance and trust us—or anyone, for that matter. Teddy Bear didn't know what the fuck was going on. She didn't know us. She didn't know you. So she weighed her options and stayed cool. Not many chicks do that these days. They wring their hands and whine. She came clean two days after meeting us. Not two years, Grudgey. Get over yourself and all your heavy-handed, holier-than-thou crap and give a kid a break. And remind me to tell you about Toni, and how she can tell if you're a lying sack o' shit by making your nose grow right on your fucking pouty face."

Cormac rolled his eyes. "Oh, c'mon, Nina. She *cannot*."

Nina strolled over, yanked a tuft of his beard and flipped him the bird. "The fuck she can't. I wish she was here right now. She'd give you hell for being such a dick to someone who's just trying to help you. Fuck, men are such pissy bitches."

Marty nodded her head in total agreement with Nina. "She can, Cormac, and she can also breathe fire. Just so's ya know."

Wanda hopped up from her place on the couch and warmed her hands by the fire. "Okay, so all this aside. The man who hired you tried to kill you last night. That's a fact. Which means he used you to find Cormac for him because you're known for your tracking abilities. How did he know to look in Colorado to begin with, is what I want to know."

"How did *you* know?" Cormac wondered out loud.

"You'll never believe us," Marty said on a grin.

"Let me guess, a crystal ball?" Cormac asked, but his tone suggested he was being a smartass.

"Ding-ding-ding-ding-ding! Winner-winner-chicken-dinner, Grizzly Adams. And don't start hollering about how we're crazy. You're a bear because some Russian dude bit your leg, okay? If you've finally swallowed that shit, Roz's crystal ball in Shamalot shouldn't be a fucking stretch. So can the disbelief and the implication we're a bunch of liars, because it damn well pisses me off," Nina ordered, reaching for a large silver bowl filled with miniature Almond Joys.

Wanda turned to face them, tucking her ivory sweater around her waist. "She's telling the truth. Take it or leave it, Cormac. I think you know my stance on your disbelief at this point. If not. I'll tell you. I'm over it. Now, the next question, how is the McDaniels fellow connected to Andre? Is he connected to him at all? Why is everyone suddenly coming out of the woodwork and trying to kill Cormac now—after three years? They have to be working toward the same goal, right?"

That made complete sense to Teddy. Maybe this Arty guy was a part of the mob, too? Or someone they paid to handle their dirty work, like a subcontractor for murder, and Cormac was the final loose end?

Wanda suddenly whipped around, her finger in the air. "Can you describe McDaniels to Cormac, Teddy? Maybe he saw him when Stas and his crew kidnapped him?"

107

As she created a picture of the man she knew as Arty McDaniels for Cormac, a beefy man with a receding hairline, thick New York accent, and penetrating black eyes, he shook his head. "There wasn't a soul with a New York accent. Everyone was Russian—or they were really good at making me believe they were Russian, with their accents."

Wanda began to pace the floor, her low-heeled, chic pumps clacking on the hardwood. "But that doesn't mean he wasn't involved. So who is this man? Why does he want Cormac, and anyone in contact with Cormac, dead? What does he have to do with the murder Toni witnessed?"

"He has to be involved with Stas. I just can't figure the connection," Teddy replied.

Cormac shook his head, jamming his hands into the pockets of his jeans. "And so what does this all mean in the end? It still means these mob guys want me dead. Now they want Teddy dead, too. Nothing changes except for how many of them we have to look out for."

"I hate to even say this out loud, but what we need to do is catch them in the act of attempted murder," Wanda said in her no-bones-about-it way.

Marty was on her feet now, too, her eyes gleaming. "But we don't just need to catch this McDaniels. We need to catch Andre, and the root of this mess, which is Stas. Don't they always say to cut the head off the dragon if you want to end its reign of terror? But how are we going to catch Stas when he sends his goons to do his dirty work? Isn't that what mob guys do? You know, like Pacino in the *Godfather*. Sort of untouchable, always giving orders, sending horse heads as threats, but never getting his hands dirty? We need to get to him somehow. Find out where he hangs out, who he socializes with, *where* he socializes. Anybody know any good Russian hangouts in Jersey?"

Teddy jumped up from the couch, panic fueling her need to move. "Here's something else to think about, too. If Andre is a bear, is Stas one, too? What about the rest of his goons? Are they all bears? Is the whole Russian contingency here in the tri-state bears? This could be much bigger than what we're capable of handling."

Wanda's lips thinned. "If it's any consolation, we've handled what some might consider worse. Maniacal genies, rogue military, vengeful demons. We've even been to Hell."

Wanda didn't appear concerned at all. Not even a little. They were sitting around, discussing this as though they were planning a murder-mystery party. These men killed without compunction, without remorse. They were diabolical killers.

But you've dealt with killers before, Teddy. You're a bounty hunter, remember?

Yeah. She was a bounty hunter. One who'd taken a real hit last year and was just now getting back on her feet.

Panic set in further. How would they ever catch a man who was capable of murder? If he was smart enough not to have been caught so far, surely he was smart enough to evade a bunch of amateurs like them.

Her phone began to chime from the pocket of her jacket, the Pointer Sisters' "We Are Family" playing a happy tune on the burner cell she always kept with her for situations just like this.

Her brothers. Probably demanding she come home—which she wasn't going to do no matter what they said. She was in this for the long haul, whether she came out of it dead or alive.

"If you're calling to demand I come home, forget it," she hissed into the phone. "I told you I was staying the course, and that's what I'm doing. No discussion. I'm a grown woman—"

"Save the I'm-an-adult speech for later, Teds, and listen carefully to me," Vadim interrupted. "We did some poking around, talked to a couple of guys who've helped us in the past."

Likely ex-cons. They had a cache of them they used from time to time as resources for all sorts of information. "And?"

"He's a cop, Teddy. Arty McDaniels is actually Carmine Ragusi. A Jersey cop with the Cherry Hill Police Department."

Chapter 10

Her heart took a nosedive to her toes as she gripped the edge of the mantle to steady her wobbling knees. "So a cop wants to get rid of Cormac? This matches up with what Cormac's sister told the people I'm with. She tried going to the police, but the day she was due to go in and talk to some detective, Toni saw him with this guy Stas."

"Speaking of Stas Vasilyev, he's some piece of shit. Has people paid off all over the tri-state. Moles everywhere. Bobby Mason gave us the story on this fuck. He's no joke, Teddy. *This* is no joke. He's a cold-blooded, no-remorse killer. Bobby says he whacked some guy just for sitting in his seat at some bar in Brooklyn. Didn't even blink an eye."

"Do you know if he's a shifter?"

"Why would you ask that?"

She explained how Cormac had been turned by Andre, to the sound of Vadim hissing in her ear.

"Look, we're coming to get you, Teds. This is big. I mean *huge*. Stas is a monster who won't think twice about killing you and he has the manpower to cover it up. The hell I'm going to let this Carmine or Stas or anyone else take one more shot at you."

The worry in Vadim's voice worried *her*. "Listen, I know your instinct is to protect me, but don't you think they'll send someone back to Colorado just as easily as they'll send someone here if they want me dead badly enough? They do know where I live. I'm not safe anywhere, Vadim."

The very words left her feeling exposed and more vulnerable than she liked admitting. There really was nowhere to hide if she hoped to avoid living the way Cormac had for three years.

"But you're safer with us. As soon as this storm clears, we're on the next flight out whether you like it or not. Do not leave that house, Teddy. Stay put. If you insist on being a part of this, then you'll just have to do it with the two of us in the mix. Now give me the address and don't give me any shit."

Closing her eyes, fighting off panic, she gave Vadim the address, almost relieved her brothers were coming to help. They were smart and resourceful, and they'd know how to help figure this out.

She'd worry about telling them the life mate thing later. Not that her life mate wanted much to do with her at this point anyway.

Clicking her phone off, she realized everyone was watching her and waiting.

"So that was my brothers, Vadim and Viktor. They contacted a couple of our resources and dug around for some information on the guy who tried to kill me last night. His name is Carmine Ragusi, and he's a cop. It's just like Toni said. The cops are in on this. According to my brothers, Stas has moles everywhere."

Cormac's head popped up, his dark hair brushing his collar as he ran his hands through the thick strands. "So there really isn't anyone we can turn to without the risk of telling the wrong people?"

Wiping her hands on her jeans, Teddy nodded. "If we choose to go to the police, we risk the chance we'll go to the wrong ones, yes."

Nina nodded her head. "Okay, so the cops are a no-go. We knew that shit anyway."

"My brothers are coming to help, if that eases your worry a little. They said they'd be on the next flight out of Colorado. They're strong and smart, and if nothing else, they'll add some strategizing and muscle to the group. They also have a lot of contacts we could probably use."

"Good to know I'll get to meet the in-laws," Cormac offered with dry sarcasm.

Okay, yes. She'd done a bad, bad thing. Yes. He should be angry she'd done a bad, bad thing. But for the love of all that was holy, was it necessary to keep pounding that home every time she spoke?

"Okay, that's enough!" Teddy hissed at Cormac and pointed at the doorway. "Kitchen, please."

She could hear Nina's cackle as she stomped into the kitchen. Spinning around, she planted her hands on the island behind her and waited for Cormac to stroll into the room.

He filled even the enormous kitchen with his presence—all muscle and ire, striding in with a look on his face that dared her to give him hell.

"Look, I apologized. And no, the mere words might not be enough right now, but the hell I'm going to grovel, got that? I did something wrong. I owned it. But I did it because I didn't know who to believe or trust either."

He rolled his tongue in his cheek. "Shouldn't you always trust your *life mate?*"

"Oh, lay the hell off, will you?" she yelped. "I know what I know, and you're my life mate. I don't understand it. I don't know how I know. I can't describe the feeling other than it's like knowing your own arm or leg. You just *know.* I can only tell you how it works when you're a bear, and this is how it works. It's how it's worked for centuries upon centuries and it's still going strong. And FYI, Crabby Gus, I don't even know how happy *I* am about it anymore either. On the life mate scale of one to ten, you've bottomed out! "

"Well, we can't have you unhappy, can we?"

That was it. That was the very moment she lost her shit.

Teddy growled just before her fist hit the countertop with a heavy thud. "Knock it off, I said! You can deal with this information however you'd like, but in the meantime, suck it. Who'd put themselves through this kind of humiliation just to save their own hide? *Who?*"

"Somebody who'd do whatever it took to see me dead?"

Teddy rose on tiptoe and stuck her face in his. "Fuck. You. Vitali. If I wanted you dead, you'd damn well be dead."

"Are you sure you and Nina aren't related?"

"Remember when you asked me if you were an asshole earlier and I cut you some slack?"

"Yep."

"Well earlier, I was *willing* to cut you some slack. You know, circumstances, long day, dart gun, just spent virtually three years alone in a cabin in the woods. But now? Right now? Not so much. Now, you're an asshole. You're the shittiest asshole that ever shit!"

Then Cormac did something completely unexpected. He laughed. Loudly, and with vigor, the hearty sound filling up the kitchen.

"How is this funny?"

He gulped for air like a fish out of water. "It's not. It's just that you're damn cute when you're angry."

Did that mean she wasn't cute when she wasn't angry? "I repeat. Fuck. You."

Cormac snorted, placing his wrist over his mouth and composing himself before he said, "Okay, okay. I'm sorry. It just hit me how ironic it is that I want to drag you over the coals for lying to me, but you're so damn cute, I can't do it."

"Is this the way you always react when there's strain in a relationship?"

"Only when the relationship involves someone as cute as you."

"Not laughing."

"That's okay, too. I can laugh for the both of us." Then he did. Laugh. Again.

Teddy nudged him in the ribs and fought a smile he didn't deserve. "Stop. We have something very serious happening here."

"Indeed we do. We just had our first argument. That done, what's next, life mate? Buying a house? Planning out our retirement?"

"Or our funerals. I like daisies. You?"

Cormac instantly sobered at that, standing up straight. "Okay, you're right. So let's get this out of the way. You lied to me. I didn't trust too many people before the ladies and you waltzed into my life. It was just me and Lenny Kravitz, the stray I found in the woods, near death. It's a knee-jerk reaction now, I guess. I just haven't had enough interaction with other human beings in the last three years to test my boundaries of trust. My reaction caught me off guard, too. Being in that cabin, hiding away like some criminal, it changed me, made me paranoid, and I'm sorry I took it out on you."

Teddy finally relaxed enough to drop down on flat feet. "Fair enough. Are we done with the snide remarks every time I open my mouth, or do you have more you'd like to unload?"

"I think I'm good for now. So here's the thing, for me anyway. I hear you telling me we're life mates. I hear you telling me this is the way of the bear, or whatever. But I'm having a lot of trouble focusing on anything other than keeping all my body parts." He held up his hand and pointed to his missing ring finger. "I'm also having trouble focusing because I'm worried that they're after you now, too. Which makes it doubly hard to do much but concentrate on saving our hides. It doesn't exactly scream romance."

So basically what he was saying was he just wasn't that into her. Sure, she was cute, and all the things she'd always been to boys. Always more their friend than their romantic interest. Why would her life mate be any different? Only *she* could rustle up a life mate who wasn't feelin' it.

"If what you're saying is we should put the life mate thing on the back burner, that's fine by me. I didn't intend for it to come out the way it did, but I had to say something while still feeling you all out because I felt cornered."

Moving in a bit closer, he asked, "So what's the deal with the life mate thing, anyway?"

"I thought we were putting it on the back burner?"

"Let's put the burner on simmer," he suggested, his words wrapped in silk.

Cormac so near made her heart pound. He smelled so good, looked so good, she found herself searching for words. "Um…well, there's a legend about mating. The legend says when you look into your mate's eyes, you'll know who's yours for eternity. I know it sounds silly, but that's how it goes."

And she hadn't believed a word of it until it happened to her.

Warmth crept up along the back of her neck and into her scalp as he used two fingers to tip her chin up. "Is that what happened to you back in Colorado after you shot me with your trusty dart gun?"

Teddy squirmed, shrugging her shoulders, finding a focal point on his shirt. "I thought we weren't addressing this part of the problem. You know, Russian mob. Death. Destruction."

"Answer the question. Is that what happened back in Colorado?"

"*Something* happened back in Colorado, yes. I haven't had time to process it all yet, okay? It's sort of like when your mom tells you the poor house is just around the corner and you roll your eyes and ignore her until you find out there really *is* a poor house, you know? I'm not telling you I'm wildly in love with you. Because I'm not. So if that's what you're thinking, relax. I'm just saying that with this information my mother bestowed upon me, I'm supposed to explore the notion that we were meant to be together. I don't know how those feelings are cultivated. The kind where we'd sacrifice our own lives for the other or whatever it is life mates do. I'm just saying, I felt something. A bond, a thread, a connection, maybe it was just attraction—"

"Me, too," Cormac interrupted, before he whispered a light kiss over the corner of her mouth, his thumb caressing her jaw with maddeningly sensuous strokes.

"What the fuck are you two doing in here? What about stone-cold killer are you nitwits missing?" Nina yelled as she hustled into the kitchen with Carl not far behind. "Quit stickin' your tongues down each other's throats and get the hell back out there where all the shit's going on! Darnell's got a line on where Stas hangs his hat and his favorite place to get snockered. "

Teddy scooted away from such close contact with Cormac, avoiding Nina's eyes by looking at the floor—which was beautiful, in all its white-and-black checkered glossy ceramic tile. "I'm sorry. We were just trying to—"

"*Who the fuck* broke my counter?" Nina shrieked, her yelp cutting and sharp. "This shit costs the earth! It's marble from Italy! This is why we can't have nice things. Greg's gonna shit a spaghetti dinner."

Teddy's eyes flew to the counter she'd slammed with her fist and they widened in horror. Sometimes she didn't know her own strength.

But Cormac was all smiles and pleasantries. "I reminded my life mate about her temper, Nina. I did. I told her, Nina's going to be mad when she sees what you've done in a fit of rage. But she was all, 'Nina-Schmina. I ain't afraid a no ex-vampire'," Cormac teased, chucking Teddy under the chin with a giggle worthy of a schoolgirl.

"Tattletale," she accused from the side of her mouth as Nina ran her hand over the very distinct fissure marring the beauty of the marble, a frown on her face. "Wow, traitor. Why not just roll the bus back over me for good measure? What happened to sacrificing your life for mine?"

"Oh, I'm not there yet, lady. In fact, I don't know if I'll ever be there enough where Nina's concerned." Then he grinned as he made a run for the doorway.

"I'm going to kick your ass, Vitali!" Teddy yelled, running after him, only for Cormac to catch her around the waist and carry her back into the living room, laughing in her ear.

And it was just another moment she could chalk up to feeling right. For now, that would have to be enough.

* * *

Cormac stood just outside one of the many turrets in Castle Nina, looking out over the skyline, the gloomy clouds gathering, mashing up against each other in an attempt at another snowstorm.

The forecast called for a possible twelve inches of precipitation, making their plans for a sting on Stas and his crew slow going.

How they were ever going to pull something off as daring as Wanda had suggested made his pulse pound in his ears. It put everyone at risk, but it especially put Teddy at risk.

He found he didn't like that much. In fact, he didn't like it at all. That bond, that connection she'd mentioned was real. He felt it, too. No, it wasn't love, but it wasn't just chemistry either. It was multifaceted, full of a kaleidoscope of muted colors as yet undefined, but ever-moving and in the process of creating shapes he knew would imprint on his heart.

He just didn't know why or how. It made no sense, but it was just like Teddy said, as logical as knowing your limbs were still attached.

This nonsensical feeling had deepened today in the kitchen while she'd defiantly told him she wasn't going to grovel for his forgiveness. He'd been pretty angry about her lie. But he'd also been angry because if she were lying, it would mean she wasn't really his life mate.

Instinctually, he knew she was telling him the truth about why she'd lied, and as she'd talked, he'd watched her beautiful lips move, her soft cheeks fill with the color of her anger, and a fragile thread had spun, attaching itself to him.

At first, he'd meant it when he said they should put this life mate thing on the back burner—there really were more important things to worry about than how they'd work out their love lives. Yet, that had changed as she explained what her mother told her.

Now, he wanted to gather her up and test out those plump lips—see if they felt as good against his as he predicted. Tug the braid from her hair and run his fingers through the glossy curtain, mold her to his body, run his hands along every curve.

But there was Toni to think of, and that thought kept him in check. She couldn't ever come back if this wasn't resolved. He wanted to see her, hear her voice, know she was safe and, above all, happy. From the way the women talked, she sure sounded happy.

"Hey. What did we tell you about big windows, targets and bullets?" Marty asked him from behind, giving him a pat on the back.

He turned around to find her smiling up at him. "Sorry. Lost in thought, I guess. This house, er, castle is really something. I was admiring the view from way up here."

"It is beautiful. My little girl Hollis loves coming here to play with Charlie and Grandpa Arch. They pretend they're princesses and Arch is their knight in shining armor. It's the cutest thing ever."

"The tight-knit network you ladies have created is to be admired."

"We have our kinks," she responded, her voice distant and laced with a sprinkle of sadness.

"You mean the kink who goes by the name of Nina?"

She flapped her hands in a dismissive gesture, pasting a smile on her face. "I'm sorry. I'm being maudlin, Cormac. I was just thinking about our children, which made me think of little Charlie and how she'll…" Her voice hitched and then she shook her head. "Forget it."

"You were thinking about how Nina won't be around for Charlie because she's no longer a vampire and her little girl is still a paranormal?" He'd thought a lot about that, too. Was his life eternal? Or just extra-long? Would he outlive everyone around him?

He hadn't found the answer in the romance novels he'd read—each author had a different take on immortality.

"A man who's perceptive. How'd that happen?" she teased, but her eyes didn't match her tone.

"I just forgot to put my Neanderthal shoes on today. It'll pass," he joked. "Though in all seriousness, I sensed your anger with her long before we formally met. Actually, I heard it."

Her hand flew to her cheek, making her bracelets jingle in the hollow hallway. "Ah, you mean all that yelling out in the woods? You're right. I *am* angry, but I don't know why. It's not even about how sluggish she is or that she's missing important things when we're involved in a case because she's so wrapped up in her food and her whatever, it's… If Nina doesn't want to be a vampire anymore, good for her. Why should I give a damn?"

"But?"

Marty plucked at her lower lip. "But she's treating it like it's some vacation. Like she was just exonerated after a life sentence in jail. Was it really so bad being a vampire? Is it really so bad for you, Cormac? I mean, it's been a long time since I was turned. I hardly remember what my life was like before I was a were."

How did you forget thinking you were crazy? The transition from human to animal? The pain of your bones distorting and crunching until you learned how to control the shift? Feeling like you were the only person in the world who'd had something as fantastically nutty happen to you?

Feeling like a total freak? Not so easily forgotten. But he'd come to a place of acceptance around year one and a half. He'd simply added it to his list of things he had no choice but to accept and make peace with.

Rocking back on his heels, Cormac was honest. "It was an adjustment I don't think I'll forget anytime soon."

Patting him on the arm, Marty chuckled. "And you did it alone. I'm sorry for that, Cormac. I can't imagine not having someone to help you go through such an enormous change. But you wait and see, my friend. By this time next year, you won't remember what your life was like without Teddy and us in it. You won't remember what it was like to be human. I promise."

He wasn't sure if she was reassuring herself or him, but her words gave him hope.

These women were confident they could handle Stas and crew. He wanted to believe them. He wanted to believe Marty, that there would actually *be* a next year.

And okay, fine. He wanted to believe there'd be a Teddy still in his life next year, too.

So there.

Chapter 11

Teddy surveyed the landscape of the kitchen table, where they'd all gathered to play Monopoly to keep their minds occupied, with a grin on her face. Lenny snuggled in her lap, contentedly purring as she slipped him bits of the salmon she and Carl had made together for lunch.

After an amazing dinner of roast leg of lamb infused with garlic and rosemary and slathered in mint jelly, small new potatoes that melted in her mouth and a Brussels sprouts casserole dripping in cheese, Wanda brought out the board games.

As the snow fell and the fire crackled, Archibald had poured them steaming cups of the homemade white chocolate cocoa he'd whipped up, topped with dollops of fresh whipped cream, and then set out plates of chocolate chip cookies fresh from the oven, and they settled in.

"I win! Park Place is *mine*, bitches!" Archibald yelped as he landed on the esteemed square, slamming his boot down with an age-spotted hand. Then he covered his mouth with his gobs money, his round, cheerful face red with embarrassment. "My apologies! Do you see what you inspire in me, Mistress Nina? You've turned me into a monster whose only goal is to beat his competition into a bloody stump! It's unforgiveable, evil woman!"

Nina slapped him on the back, her cackling laughter filling the room. "Aw, c'mon, Arch. It's good for your heart to get your gloat on."

He gasped and shook his wad of money at her with an admonishing look. "It is most assuredly not a sign of good sportsmanship to behave in such a manner, Nina Statleon. That you encourage such is despicable!"

"You know you wanna make it rain, Arch. Go on," she taunted him, pointing to the play money.

He cleared his throat, brushing a hand over his ascot as though Nina had suggested he strip naked and hula hoop. "I most certainly do not wish to make it, as you say, *rain*."

"Do toooo!" And then Nina began to chant, "Make it rain! Make it rain!"

Soon, they were all pounding their fists on the table and encouraging the manservant.

Archibald suddenly grinned, saucy and devilish, hopping up from the table and pushing his chair away. "Fine then, you heathens. I do admit to hoping against eternal hope there would come a time when I could bellow, 'In your face.' On that admission, in your face, homie!" he shouted, fanning the money on his palm and shooting it at Nina with deft fingers, making it flutter to the floor as he did a little dance.

Teddy laughed so hard, she almost cried, her body leaning into Cormac, who howled with laughter, too. That was the moment she realized how long it had been since she'd just hung out with people for the sake of hanging out. Enjoyed someone else's company other than the animals at Sanctuary. Accepted an invitation to have a beer with her coworkers.

When had she become so fond of isolation?

You know when, Teddy Bear. You know why. But this is nice, isn't it? Cooking with Carl today. Chatting with Marty about what color best suits you. Listening to Nina and Wanda share stories about some of their OOPS adventures. Sure, there's a dark cloud hanging over your head, but there's a life you've been missing. You accused Cormac of isolating himself, but you did the same thing. You just weren't in a cabin in the woods. You were in your bedroom at the ranch or in your office at Sanctuary or in that prison in your head. Not so different than Cormac after all.

And then there was Cormac himself, and all these new feelings he kept stirring in her. How just his lips against hers for no more than a second left her yearning for more—for something she was still so unclear about.

Her phone signaled a text, interrupting the retrospective on her pathetic, cloistered life. As she pulled it out of her pocket, Cormac rested his chin on her shoulder and watched her read the bad news from her brothers.

"Damn," she muttered, looking up at everyone. "My brothers are snowed in and can't get a flight out." Shit. Shit. Shit. They needed as much manpower as necessary if they were going to manage to get to Stas.

And then another text popped up.

One that made her gulp.

Her hand squeezed the phone with a shaky grasp. The universe had a bone to pick with her, it seemed. But now just wasn't the time to add more fuel to the fire.

"Who's Dennis?" Cormac asked against her ear.

She set Lenny on Cormac's lap and pushed her chair from the table. "I have to use the ladies' room. Excuse me."

Teddy didn't bother to look back to see Cormac's reaction to her abrupt departure or to see if anyone else noticed. She needed air. Crisp, clean, cold air, filling her lungs, reminding her to just breathe.

Blindly, she made her way out of the kitchen and stumbled down the long hall where a door led to a small courtyard just outside the hedge maze. She'd found it earlier today, and now she was grateful. All she needed was cool air and a moment to gather her thoughts, rein in her fear enough to keep it together.

Pushing open the door, she poked her head outside and sniffed, at least thinking enough to look for danger before she stepped into the snow and pulled the door shut behind her.

The moon was brilliant in the sky, buttery yellow in the velvet ink of night, casting a peaceful glow over the entrance to the hedge maze. A light snow continuously fell, white flakes sticking to the boxwood hedges that made up the maze, sugaring the tops of them with crystal flecks.

The covered patio made of white stone and swirly circles of some kind of crushed blue and green mosaic tile would be beautiful to sit on and while a day away under normal circumstances. Tonight, the beauty of the craftsmanship and time put into creating a masterpiece like this escaped her.

There was a black wrought iron chair she shook the snow from before she sat down and put her head between her knees, inhaling, letting the frigid air cleanse her.

Dennis was on the loose again. This could only mean one thing.

She didn't just have the Russian mob knocking at her door—she had the man who'd almost killed her last year likely hunting her down, too. And Dennis *would* hunt her down. She knew it as sure as the day was long. He'd never let her get away with putting him in jail, even if his stay hadn't been nearly as long as it should have been.

He would find a way to find her—wherever she went.

Yanking her phone from her pocket, she reread the text from Vadim. *Dennis is out of jail. Word in certain circles is he's asking questions about you. You have to tell everyone about him so they can protect you. Stay where you are until we can get to you.*

Her disgust crept up along her spine as she scrunched her eyes shut. Eight months for assault and battery was hardly the kind of punishment Dennis deserved for leaving her unconscious in a ravine, where she would have bled out had it not been for Vadim and Viktor finding her in time.

Teddy's chest tightened when she remembered Dennis's eyes just before he'd round-housed her in the face, knocking her a hundred feet to the forest below them. There was hatred in his eyes, thick, black, and rich with evil.

"Teddy?"

She gasped out loud, gripping the cold wrought iron arms on the chair before she realized it was Cormac. Her heart raced, pounding inside her chest. Damn. Noises that startled her had been one of her biggest phobias to overcome since that night in the forest.

But he gripped her shoulder with a strong, warm hand. "Sorry, didn't mean to scare you." He came to stand in front of her before sitting on his haunches and gripping her cold hands. "You know you shouldn't be out here in the open. You okay?"

"Yes. I'm fine. Just needed some air. Bears are unusually warm creatures—especially females—which is why Florida's out, in case that was your dream retirement spot," she joked. Hoping her voice sounded as light as she'd tried to keep it.

"Good to know. I was never much for sand in my shorts. Plus, I know I don't look like it, but underneath all this hair on my face, I'm a little pasty."

Teddy snickered, trying to relax.

"So who's Dennis?"

And there it was. The big lead elephant in the room. She had no choice but to tell him. They hadn't touched on their prior relationships at this point, so she figured it could wait until they took the life mate thing off the back burner, but with Dennis loose…

Clearing her throat, Teddy gripped his wide hands, calloused and warm. "He's my ex-husband. He just got out of prison for assault and battery."

Cormac's face darkened as his eyes searched hers. "You were married?"

"For two years, until I knew better." Two hellish years she'd spent coddling him, making excuses for him, allowing him to berate her, belittle her and, in the end, verbally lash her at every turn until his verbal abuse turned into domestic violence.

Tilting her chin up, he asked, "Were you going to tell me?"

She sighed, the cold air escaping her mouth in a puffy cloud. "Eventually. This wasn't something I purposely kept from you. I've gotten good at my mental block where Dennis is concerned. And he wasn't even a concern until tonight. I just didn't think I had to say anything yet, seeing as we were putting everything life mate on the back burner."

"So just a quick question before we go any further. If I'm your life mate, why did you marry Dennis?"

"Well, one, because I wasn't sure I believed the legend, and two, in the beginning, he was a lot of fun. Charming, funny…"

"And then?"

"And then I became his punching bag. At first he just verbally beat me down. Gaslighted me every time he had the chance, leading me to believe I was crazy. Then it became physical and that's when I left."

That last night with Dennis before she'd finally thrown in the towel would always be an ugly reminder of how not to end a relationship. She'd asked for a divorce, and he'd almost choked her to death.

Cormac's hands stiffened, the muscles in his forearms flexing. "He hit you?" His voice rang with the kind of disbelief only a man with true integrity would.

"He almost killed me," she confessed, squashing a sob.

The road to recovery since that night had been long. The physical journey had been a snap. It was the mental trip she'd gone on that had knocked her for a loop and left her scrambling to regain her life, in the way an act so violent can do to you.

He brushed her hair from her cheek with the back of his hand, his next question gentle. "Okay, so I know this is going to sound like a ridiculous question in the midst of something so difficult, but how could he have almost killed you if you self-heal?"

"There are so many things you don't know, I forget. When Dennis came after me because I'd filed for a divorce, I was on a bounty. He tracked me and found me out in the forest, and then beat me to hell and back. Broke my ribs, my collarbone, fractured my pelvis, and yes, those are all things that would self-heal, but when he kicked me over the side of a ravine, I was

126

knocked unconscious. Your healing slows when you're down for the count because you need to concentrate on the healing. I dropped about a hundred feet and landed on a sharp rock, and punctured my lung. If my brothers hadn't found me when they did, I would have bled out."

"Jesus Christ," Cormac hissed, kneeling in the snow and pulling her into a tight embrace, his arms secure and warm around her. "I'm sorry. You don't have to say any more. Just forget I asked."

Curling her head into his shoulder, she squeezed her eyes shut. Not because Dennis evoked tears anymore, her eyes had long since dried out over him. But because they didn't need this added stress in an already strained situation.

Still, that wasn't the only reason. She didn't want to remember how hard it had been to trust herself again, her instincts, her ability to judge another's character.

"This really screws up everything, huh?"

Cormac set her from him and gave her a look of confusion. "What?"

"Now I'm not just looking over my shoulder for one bad guy who wants my head on a platter, I'm looking for two."

Gripping her shoulders, he narrowed his eyes in the darkness. "And you think that's somehow your fault?"

"Well, it sure doesn't help. I did marry the man."

"You know what doesn't help, Teddy? You blaming yourself because some asshole beat you almost to death and now he's free to do it again. *How* in the hell is that your fault?"

Without thinking, without even breathing, she gripped either side of his shirt and kissed him. Kissed him hard, smoothing her hands up over his broad chest to bracket his face. She kissed him because he'd accepted her answers without hesitation.

Cormac's tongue slid into her mouth, stroking her own, the heat of the silken rasp against hers leaving her dizzy. His beard, crisp and coarse, scraped against her cheeks with delicious friction. The kiss deepened, becoming heated, their breathing harsh as their chests met.

He scooped her up, pulling her tight to him until they were standing, backing her against the house so the brick wall met her spine and then he melted into her, his rigid body, every muscle, every sculpted line pressed into her.

Cormac's arms snaked around her, his hand splaying over her ass, pulling her deeper, closer, until there was nothing but the sound of their harsh breathing and their mouths, devouring one another's.

The door popping open made them both jump, but not apart; rather, they clung to one another tighter.

Carl's dark head poked out of the heavy door, his lopsided grin in place when he flipped the light on. He motioned them inward, the duct tape holding his index finger on shiny under the bright patio light. "Insiiide, pease," he said.

"Hey, Carl," Cormac replied with a warm smile. "We'll be right in, okay? Go tell Nina and the others, would ya?"

Carl nodded, his grin widening, and then he pointed to the watch at his wrist, which in zombie-speak she'd learned meant hurry it up.

Teddy cleared her throat and nodded her head, smiling back at him. "We'll hurry, promise. Get in there now so you don't catch your death...er, I mean a cold. Wait. Can zombies catch a cold?"

Carl snickered and shut the door, leaving them to deal with what she'd just done.

"I'm sorry," she murmured, unable to look Cormac in the eye.

"Your words, they cut like a knife."

"Huh?"

"Are you sorry you kissed me? Because I'm fragile right now, and I'm pretty sure if you tell me you're sorry you kissed me, I'll flat-out break," he teased, letting his lips graze her jaw.

Shivering, Teddy shook her head and shrugged. "I'm not sorry I kissed you. I meant I'm sorry I was so abrasive. You telling me I wasn't to blame just struck a sensitive place. I guess I got overwhelmed. I don't know. I kissed you, okay?"

He grinned and winked. "Yeah, it was pretty okay. And damn right it's not your fault. Listen, if the Teddy I'm coming to know is anything like I think she is, you blamed yourself for sticking it out for so long with Dennis, am I right?'

Oh, the endless nights of blame, of reliving all the moments she should have walked out the door and never looked back. "I stayed too long."

"So you suppose the length of time would have changed the outcome of the end of your marriage? Do you suppose Dennis just wouldn't have beaten you almost to death if you'd done it sooner?"

"You're probably right."

"No. I am right, Teddy. *I am right*. This fuck's an abusive prick. He would have been just as angry had you left a few months into the marriage as he would have in a couple of years. And it's damn well not your fault he got out of jail."

"I still can't believe his attorney managed to reduce the charges from attempted murder to assault and battery and jail time. But his parents have a lot of money and a lot of heavy-duty contacts in Denver."

"Yeah, I can't believe it either. But *you* can believe, if he shows up, the murder won't be an attempt."

Putting her fingers to his lips, she shook her head. "He doesn't know where I am, and my brothers are aware he's out. They'll keep an eye out and if he so much as sneezes too loud, they'll see to it he's right back in jail. I don't want you involved in this, Cormac. This is my baggage."

"I'm sorry, isn't it mine, too? You know, life mates and sacrifices and all?"

Jabbing a finger into his shoulder, Teddy giggled. "I'm sorry, weren't you the one who gave me up to Nina to save your own pretty hide?"

He made a face. "Well, c'mon. Be fair. Nina's damn frightening. I don't care if she's not a vampire anymore. She's just as intimidating as a human. I had no choice but to hand you over. Who wants their face chewed off?"

Teddy's head fell back on her shoulders as she laughed. "She's a formidable foe even human. I agree."

Leaning down, he brushed her lips with his once more, leaving her almost breathless. "We'd better get back inside before that foe decides we're the enemy. But let's discuss this more in depth later, okay?"

She shot him a warm smile, her toes curling inside her boots. "Done deal."

Gripping her hand, he pulled her back inside and they were traversing the long hallway again when she heard Nina yelp, "That son of a motherfucking bitch!"

Cormac and Teddy exchanged glances as they followed the sound of the television to the family room, where everyone had gathered.

Sectional couches in plush fabric were scattered throughout the wide room, where the focal point was an eighty-inch flat screen.

With both she and Cormac's faces flashing on it in vivid colors.

"What the hell is going on now?" Teddy almost shrieked.

"I'll tell you what the hell," Nina said from clenched teeth. "That fuck-knuckle Carmine Ragusi went on live friggin' TV and accused the two of you of murder."

Chapter 12

The hits just kept on comin', was Teddy's first thought, second only to the sheer terror a murder charge with she and Cormac's names attached to it brought.

"Murder?" Cormac thundered, dropping her hand and moving closer to the television as the reporter was just wrapping up the story.

"That's what I said—murder," Nina groused, rewinding the broadcast so they could watch for themselves.

As the reporter replayed the interview with that lying sack of smelly shit Arty, aka Carmine Ragusi, her knees threated to give out.

Carl came up behind her, driving his hands around her waist and squeezing her. "You are niii…ce."

She shuddered out a breath and gripped his hands, fighting a sting of tears at how sensitive he was to everyone around him. His hands were cold, but they were comforting just the same.

So now the story was Carmine Ragusi believed his partner had something on Cormac and Teddy, and Carmine had some kind of evidence to prove they'd killed his partner? Without a body?

Whoa. Her head was spinning.

Teddy's mouth went dry when she was finally able to speak. "How?" she managed to push out.

Wanda was on her feet in an instant, tucking her light sweater around her waist and approaching Teddy with worried eyes. "We think that's who was murdered the night Toni found Stas and Andre standing next to a dead guy. He was Carmine Ragusi's partner at the precinct. He needs someone to take the fall for his dead partner."

"That's insane." Cormac's jaw had gone stiff, his fist balled into a wad of anger.

Marty buzzed about them, too, her wheels spinning, her hands waving. "We have a theory. Carmine's partner, whose name was Mauricio Benneducci, by the way, caught Carmine in the thick of this Russian mob thing and they took him out to keep his mouth shut. I'd bet all my lip gloss Carmine was at the dealership that night and he was the one who killed Mauricio. Toni may not have seen him there. Maybe he left. Or maybe he was hiding and waiting to kill Toni when she showed her face. Thank God she got away when she did. But I'd also bet Stas *ordered* Carmine to kill his partner because in this nut Stas's mind, Carmine was to blame for his partner finding out he was on the take. Stas and Carmine had to be worried about how much Cormac knew after finding Toni with him. Cormac being a loose end like that is bad for Stas. So, Teddy, you were probably right when you said Carmine just needed you to find Cormac and the plan all along was to kill you, too. No one was supposed to know anything about Cormac or Toni to begin with. Eliminating you, and probably your brothers, would have shut that right down."

"Hold on," Cormac interjected. "There were no deaths or murders reported on the night Toni witnessed the murder at the dealership, or even in the vicinity, and not a single word of one from that night since this all happened. I've gone over the blotters for every single arrest hundreds of times. If Ragusi killed his partner—a cop, no less—why wasn't there some kind of all-out manhunt? He was a cop, for Christ's sake! Cops stick together, don't they?"

Marty pressed a hand to Cormac's arm and nodded, her logical tone a small consolation in this mess. "Here's what we think. Yes, the cops would have let loose the hounds of hell to find who killed one of their own, but that's only if they thought Mauricio was *dead*. Maybe Carmine somehow managed to make them believe there was suspicion surrounding his partner's mental health or whatever. Sure, they'd look high and low for him, but you weren't looking for a missing cop, Cormac. You were looking for dead bodies."

Teddy was still trying to make sense of being a suspect in a murder. "How can they do this without a body? Where the *hell* is Mauricio Benneducci's body?"

Marty's lips thinned. "Carmine's a cop, and I'd bet he's pretty convincing when presenting the police with everything they need to at least investigate you two. I can only imagine the tale he spun, but you can be sure it's a damn good one. They don't need a body to question you surrounding the disappearance of a police officer, honey. And Carmine doesn't need a body to get you out in the open. This is all an effort to smoke you two out. It's a huge risk for him to take. I mean, what if other cops find you first—cops who aren't dirty? He's obviously pretty desperate at this point."

Cormac dragged his hand through his hair. "We need Toni here. There has to be a way to get her here. She could tell us if this Mauricio is the guy she saw in a pool of blood that night."

Wanda pressed her fingers to her temples and winced. "The door to the other realm can only be opened during certain times of the full moon cycle and some star configuration. I can't remember the exact circumstances, but I do remember I have it on the calendar in my phone and it's another month away."

"Jesus," Cormac muttered.

Teddy's stomach sank, the butterflies from earlier replaced with sick dread. "So this Carmine's effectively turned the tables on us. He's plastered our faces all over the news nationwide."

The kind of balls this took meant he was either desperate or he had some kind of death wish.

Cormac ran his hand through his hair again and sighed. "I'd love to know what this evidence is. The son of a bitch."

Nina scoffed, her face twisted up in a scowl. "Well, you heard what the reporter said. He just miraculously uncovered it. You know the media score. They're billing it like it's some startling revelation, eatin' it up like stray dogs. It also means the pansy fuck is scared because Teddy can identify him."

"But he knows where we are, Nina!" Cormac returned, his fists clenched. "He knows where Teddy is. Why does he have to smoke us out?"

Wanda nodded her head in Darnell's direction. "Because of our resident demon."

Nina cackled her pleasure. "Some demon shit—a spell or whatever. Nobody can get in or out of the grounds now. I had him do it last night after the dude took a shot at Teddy. But you two can't hide fucking forever. We need to handle this shit quick."

Reaching for the back of one of the recliners, Teddy had to hold on to it to keep her knees from collapsing out from under her and knocking Carl down. "So what do we do now? We obviously can't leave here if there's a manhunt for alleged cop killers." She knew she sounded hysterical, but she wasn't used to being on this side of the law.

Nina nudged her shoulder with a light fist. "Here's what we do—we chill the fuck out and we think about our plan of attack. If Carmine Ragusi wants to fucking play, then we play. For right now, you're safe here. He's not givin' you two up—not yet anyway. It buys us a little time to find a way to make him and that borscht-loving freak Stas confess."

This was hopeless. A guy like Stas wasn't confessing to anything ever. *Ever.*

"It's late, Teddy, and you look exhausted. Why not try to get some sleep and let us worry about the rest for now?" Marty suggested, wrapping her arm around Teddy's waist and squeezing.

Her eyes widened in disbelief. "Are you kidding me? I'll never sleep with a murder charge hanging over my head."

"You haven't been charged with anything, honey. Neither of you have. You're just suspects in an investigation," Wanda reminded her, her tone sympathetic.

"We might as well be on *America's Most Wanted* or the back of milk cartons at this point. I don't see how we can get a confession out of Stas, short of threatening to kill him."

"If that's how we gotta roll, that's how we gotta roll," Nina said without pause.

Before Teddy could protest the idea of murder, and the cold chill along her spine that came with it, Archibald swept in, two mugs in his hands with tendrils of steam winding out of them. "Miss Theodora, I've made you my special brew. Guaranteed to help you get a restful night's sleep. You as well, Master Cormac. Now drink up, children—the sandman awaits."

Both Teddy and Cormac took the mugs from Archibald with skeptical eyes. She didn't plan on sleeping for at least a hundred years, but if it made Archibald happy, someone who'd welcomed them into the fold, cooked and cleaned as though they were his own, no way would she insult him.

He swept his hands in a shooing motion. "Off with you both now. Fresh sheets and warm blankets are on your beds in the basement, as well as clean nightwear. Pleasant dreams," he said with that twinkling smile, escorting them out of the TV room and toward the basement door.

She turned at the head of the steps and impulsively hugged Archibald, letting the scent of fresh vanilla and cookies on his pristine jacket soothe her. "Thank you, Archibald. You've been very kind to us on such short notice."

"'Tis nothing, Theodora. You're always welcome wherever I go. Sleep well, lovely lady." He dropped a kiss on her cheek and nodded to Cormac. "You as well, Master Cormac. Tomorrow, we slay the dragon!" he shouted as he took his leave.

As they made their way down the stairs, a warm glow of light shining from a small lamp, she had to admit, the bed did look pretty inviting.

They were silent as they took turns changing behind the princess privacy screen with knights on horses and princesses with long, flowing hair, waving from castle turrets.

They each finally sat at the edge of their respective beds and sipped the warm brew Archibald gave them.

Both silent.

Both lost in their own thoughts.

* * *

"Wow. Wow. Wow," Cormac murmured sleepily, the rustle of the sheets as he repositioned himself meeting her ears.

Teddy giggled from her bed. Yeah. Wow. She felt great. Better than she had in well over a year. "What the heck was in that special brew?"

"I dunno, but unicorn sighting at three o' clock."

"You think that looks like a unicorn? I was leaning more toward Clydesdale."

"We're sharing hallucinations?"

"It's what life mates do."

Cormac barked a weak laugh. "Whatever's in that tea, I want a permanent port put in my arm filled with it. I haven't been this relaxed in forever."

She nodded, tucking the comforter under her chin as she drifted on a fluffy cloud. "It's pretty great."

"You feel better now?"

"As good as any murder suspect feels, I suppose."

"Let's not talk about that. Let's talk about something else."

"You wanna name your unicorn?"

Cormac chuckled. "How about we get to know each other?"

"You mean like whether I want the top or bottom bunk in our cell? What our prison pet names should be? That kind of intimate detail sharing?"

"Aw, c'mon, Teddy Bear, play nice. No talk of prison or dirty cops or murder. Deal?"

She closed her eyes and a cornucopia of colors rushed past her eyelids; she smiled. "Hmmm-mmm. Deal."

"So tell me everything about Teddy."

"Bra-size everything or favorite-color everything?"

"How about we start with favorite color?"

"Yellow."

"I'm green."

"Green is nice."

"Okay, scratch favorite colors. It's superficial and boring and the only time I'll need to know what your favorite color is will be when we pick out paint for our house. Let's go deeper. Ask me something you've been wondering about since we met and I'll do the same."

"Okay, in the interest of going deeper, how did you deal with becoming a bear? I mean, how did you learn to shift and…I dunno, the million and one things that come with such an enormous life change? I've been going over how crazy that must have been and I can't wrap my head around the idea."

"Romance novels," he said, deadpan.

"Come again?"

"I read romance novels, and I'll have you know, this tea makes my lips loose."

"Romance novels? Please, please, *pleeease* explain."

"Promise you won't laugh?"

"Nope."

"Fine. You were bound to find out anyway. So when this all went down, there wasn't like a guide on how to become a bear or anything. So I Googled all sorts of crazy phrases like 'going from human to bear' and 'shape shifting' etcetera. That led me to romance novels. Just an FYI, we're huge in romance."

She knew she should be alarmed by the idea that everything he knew about being a bear shifter he'd learned in a romance novel, but he was still standing. That said something for romance novels and vivid imaginations.

"Bears are?"

"Last year we were all the rage. Right up there with vampires."

"Okay, so you read romance novels and that taught you about the shift?"

"Yep. I read a bunch of Eve Langlais and some other folks with catchy titles like *Bearly There*. Billionaire bears, alpha bears. You name it, I read it. That's where I started and it went from there. Tons of reading material, tons of different takes on bear shifting. Some not so far off the mark, if what you say is true."

Now she really laughed. "Promise me something?"

"What's that?"

"Never ever tell a single soul how you learned how to shift. Ever."

"Will they laugh me out of the clan?"

"You could lose your man cred. And it's the sleuth. We have sleuths they'll laugh you out of, not clans."

"Oh, right. A group of us are called sleuths. Don't think I ever came across that term."

"It's kinda old school. So the first shift—how horrible was that?"

He blew out a breath. "The scariest shit I've ever experienced in my whole life, bar none. Even Stas and his thugs don't compare to that."

"I'm sorry, Cormac. How awful to have gone through that all alone."

"I'll never forget seeing myself in a mirror after that first shift. Jesus..." he muttered.

She couldn't even imagine it. It had been hard enough as a cub with plenty of parental support, but all alone? It had to be terrifying. "The shift is a big deal in our circles, just so you know. Had anyone known, there would have been a ceremony, blessings, all sorts of good things."

"Kind of like a Bar Mitzvah only with honey and salmon?"

"And a big disco ball for dancing after all the rituals are complete."

Cormac laughed again. "I'm damned put out that I missed doing the Chicken Dance. But somehow I managed. It turned out all right."

Cormac had to have some kind of will to survive, doing that all on his own. His determination spoke to his character and it made her toes tingle.

"But to not understand what was happening to your body, to wonder if you'd always be like this? Not knowing any of the things involved with a shift—not to mention our lifestyles, what we need to survive. That we don't hibernate like non-shifter bears. The details of being a shifter that you have no idea about. That sucks. On behalf of all of my fellow bear shifters, I apologize."

"I will say this, once I got past the whole similarities to *Teen Wolf*, it was a little cool. But there was a long period of time where I went through the 'I'm a freak' stage."

Her heart clenched in sympathy, making her hands tighten around the sheets. "So how did you end up at that cabin? It's so far out of the way of everything. Like really deep into the forest."

"I got damn lucky. I don't know who it belonged to before me or how long it's been there, but it was there like a mirage in a sandy desert. I watched for days before I got up the guts to move in. After that, I pieced the kitchen and bedroom together by Dumpster diving at night in the nearest town."

"And Lenny? I love Lenny Kravitz. So he was a stray?"

Cormac's voice warmed the darkness surrounding them. "I found him half frozen on one of my treks around the perimeter of the cabin. Poor little guy, I didn't think he'd make it. But I wasn't giving up. He was the first contact I had with anything other than the typical animals in the forest."

"And his name—how'd that happen?"

"Have you seen my cat's swagger? He's the epitome of cool. Just like Lenny. But now look at him. One can of salmon from Nina and he's sleeping with her on her California king. Traitor."

Teddy chuckled, closing her eyes. "She does have an uncanny way with animals, and situations like Carl's, where her need to nurture is probably some of the best mothering I've ever seen."

"Did you catch her reading to him? It was pretty great. I'd have never guessed she was as patient as she was until she and Carl sat down before dinner to read, of all things, Jane Austen. It's incredible."

"They're all pretty incredible." Every last one of them. She liked them far more than she'd ever liked anyone in just a couple of days' worth of time spent together. She liked their vibe, their interaction, their loyalty and even their bickering.

"I'm coming to see that. I think they're the most selfless people I've ever met. They're balls to the wall, all in. I'm beyond grateful Toni had them."

Something she'd wondered about since she found out everything began in Jersey made her ask, "How did you get to Colorado all the way from Jersey? Especially after being bitten?"

"This will sound weird, but after I was bitten, I staggered around for probably a week, sleeping in rest areas and trying to conserve the cash I still had on me."

Teddy gasped, fighting a yawn. "Stas didn't rob you blind? What kind of murderer is he anyway?"

"Apparently the kind who only likes removing body parts. But I wondered about that, too. I couldn't believe my wallet was still in my back pocket; everything exactly like it was when they knocked me out and took me. I just knew I had to get somewhere safer than Jersey. I must've called Toni a million times from various burner cells, only to fill up her voice mail with messages. I swear, I thought she was dead. I was convinced she was dead."

The anguish in his voice forced her to ask, "Why didn't you go just to the police when you got away, Cormac? Report Toni missing? Surely they would have at least investigated. Tell them about how they held you hostage and chopped off your finger?"

"Because when they thought I was unconscious, I listened to them joke about all the cops and the city administrators on their payroll. I knew damn well they couldn't be trusted."

"Just like what Toni experienced," Teddy whispered. Christ, what a rock and a hard place for him to land between.

"Yep," he said on a yawn. "I became so paranoid, I started to wonder if I should trust myself."

"And Colorado? How did you get all the way to my home state from Jersey?"

"You'll laugh."

"Did you read it was the place to find other bear shifters in one of your romance novels?"

"Hah! No. It was instinctual. That's the only way to describe it. After I stumbled around, trying to figure out if Toni was dead or alive, spent day after day in one homeless shelter or another, hatching plans to find just one damn cop who wasn't corrupt and wouldn't think I was out of my mind, I was losing hope fast. So I did what some might consider stupid. I took out a bunch of cash advances from my credit cards, leaving a big fat trail of where I'd been. My credit is obliterated by now. But I needed cash if I hoped to get anywhere or buy technology I could use to research these nuts. Also, I don't know if you noticed, but bears need to eat. Often. The soup kitchen wasn't cutting it in terms of addressing my hunger."

"Wait until you see me mow down a seventy-two ounce Porterhouse in less than twenty minutes. Then we'll talk about appetites."

"You're making me all gushy and tingly," he teased, his voice enveloping her like a warm blanket. "Anyway, Colorado just came to me one night. I was probably at my lowest point. I was cold, tired, hungry, hadn't showered in days, and the wound from Andre's bite had all but disappeared. So I was freaked about that, too."

"So you still hadn't experienced the shift?"

"Nah. That almost happened on the bus to Colorado."

That made her eyes fly open. "Oh my God!"

Cormac groaned. "Yeah. Tell me about it. Anyway, I was low—really low. I fell asleep at some point, but sleep had become really restless, my dreams were always weird and broken. But this night, I guess it all got to me and I passed out cold at a rest area on the border of Pennsylvania. But I was startled awake by what I thought was someone yelling in my ear. All I remember was the word Colorado, clear as a bell, and from that moment on, there was this crazy drive to get there at all costs. So I bought a bus ticket, and here I am."

"You'll probably say this sounds nuts, but there's a legend amongst us bears, you know. One that says you'll find where your roots should grow when the spirit of an aimless wanderer shouts it in your ear in a dream. That's how I knew going back to Colorado after college in Utah was the right thing for my life's path"

"If he's aimless, how come he's giving advice on directions?"

Rolling to her side, Teddy smiled, tucking the pillow beneath her cheek. "That's why he's so good. Because he spent his living years roaming aimlessly, looking for all the good spots. At least that's what my mom told me. He's like your personal GPS."

"Through the entire ordeal, it was the smartest move I could have made. Going to Colorado gave me the chance to catch my breath, get my feet under me. Meet you…"

Her heart skipped at least three beats. "I darted you. You couldn't possibly mean that." But she hoped he did.

"Teddy?"

"Yeah?"

"If I could actually get out of this bed without feeling like I'd just polished off an entire bottle of JD, and I was sure I wasn't going to drool all over your pretty face, I'd kiss you. I'd kiss the hell out of you."

She fought a sigh. The biggest, girliest sigh ever. "If I thought my lips would cooperate rather than feel like two rubbery worms at war with one another, I'd kiss you back," she said, a little breathless.

"Maybe we should save it for our first date. Like official date. Nice clothes, nice restaurant with a big Porterhouse, no pressure from the kill squad. Like prom, but not."

"I never went to prom," slipped from her lips without warning.

God, why had she admitted that? It only made her sound pathetic.

"*What?* How could someone as beautiful as you miss out on a hot dress, spiked punch, a kitschy theme, and some guy with hands like an octopus, mauling you half to death?"

She giggled into her hand. "Just lucky, I guess? Though seriously, my mom died when I was just hitting my teens. My brothers don't know prom dress from a pile of horse dung. They were young when they took on the responsibility of raising me, and back then, we didn't have a lot of money to go around. I didn't have the heart to ask them to spend it on a dress when it was hard enough just getting food on the table. So I skipped it. Besides, nobody asked."

"Well, we'll just have to see what we can do about that," he murmured, though it was likely just empty words from Archibald's special brew. "Date?"

As her eyes closed and sleep began to creep in, Teddy nodded. "Definitely a date."

"Night, Teddy. Sweet dreams," his whispered, his husky voice lazy and comforting.

"You, too…"

When she finally succumbed to sleep, she dreamt of floaty prom dresses made of tulle and sparkly things, balloons in pastel colors enveloping her and Cormac, drifting past them on a dance floor, where they clung to one another and swayed to a soft ballad.

Right in the middle of her dream, she decided it was probably the sweetest of dreams she'd ever had.

Chapter 13

"I feel like my stomach's about to explode," Marty complained, yanking at the hem of her ultra-short dress, which made her figure look like she'd popped right out of a magazine for curvy women.

She was stunning in the slinky black Lycra that covered her from chin to mid-thigh like a sleek glove, and if the information Toni had once given to Marty during their many conversations about Stas, she should have no problem getting his attention.

"That's because your fat ass is warring with your gut," Nina said on a cackle as she shoveled a freshly baked frozen pizza in her mouth next to Lenny, who was happily eating yet another can of salmon.

Marty's lips thinned. "Shut up and mind your own P's and Q's. Shouldn't you be washing your driving gloves or something, *chauffer?*"

Nina planted the heels of her hands on the counter of the kitchen island and leaned over, growling. "I said I'd go in. I can do more than just drive. I told you, just because I'm fucking human, doesn't mean I can't still handle some shit."

"With what? Your fierce glare of death and your awkward, slower-than-an-act-of-congress ninja moves? You stay in the car where you damn well belong, Nina. You are not a vampire anymore. I repeat, *not a vampire!*"

Wanda dropped a red duffel bag on the island between them with a loud thunk meant to startle the two women she called friends. "Not today, girls. Hear me? We all have to focus on our jobs. No arguing over anything or I swear, I'll personally rip your vocal chords from your creamy throats. We each have tasks. Tasks that are best suited to our abilities. We will perform said task without a peep of dissention. Now knock it off. We're all on edge. This is it. This is our chance to finally get Cormac out from under this damn dark cloud that's been hovering over his head and reunite him with Toni. *Don't screw it up.*"

Archibald cleared his throat as he entered the kitchen and sauntered across the floor like a runway model. He wore a pinstriped suit in a deep navy blue, double breasted, coupled with a black shirt and a white tie and a matching fedora.

He was just shy of a Tommy gun and cigar.

Arch did a little twirl and winked his eye at the women, followed by a saucy smile.

Nina wolf-whistled at him. "Every girl's crazy 'bout a sharp-dressed man, Gansgta!" she whooped.

"I take it you approve, ladies?" he asked on a bow.

Wanda gave him one of those fond smiles she was always doling out, but she shook her head in admonishment. "We're not going after Jimmy Hoffa, Arch. They're Russian mobsters, not *The Sopranos*."

Arch scoffed at her, clicking his heels together. "It never hurts to dress the part, Lady Wanda. How could I possibly pass up a hat as smart as this one? If I'm to be in charge of keeping our former mistress of the dark on task and in our getaway car, it can only benefit me to get into character."

Marty rolled her eyes with a chuckle and squeezed his arm. "You be careful, you hear me, Arch? Ex-Elvira's a crafty one. She'll pull out all the stops to stick her nose in where it doesn't belong. Make sure she stays put in the getaway car. No varying from the plan."

Nina ripped a piece of her pizza off and chewed, jamming her middle finger up at Marty.

Darnell strolled in then, his wide grin and big personality sweeping through the kitchen and warming Teddy. He fist-bumped with Carl before yanking the zombie into a bear hug.

"Do you have what we need, D?" Wanda asked as she pulled on a pea coat and dark knit cap, completely changing her overall appearance and air of sophistication to one of anonymity.

"Yes'm." He drove his beefy hand into his Giants jacket and pulled out a recording device Cormac had sent him to purchase.

"And you've located this bar the freak hangs out in with his goons?"

"Yep, an' I got the dude's cell number, too. A direct hotline to the bad guy. All right up in here." He pointed to his head.

"Up top, Demon," Wanda said on a smile, holding her hand up in the air for him to high-five her.

As they all prepared to put into motion this sting they'd concocted while she and Cormac slept the sleep of the dead after drinking Arch's special brew, Teddy fought the urge to scream.

Everyone was laughing and joking and chatting as though they'd done this a hundred times. Like they were role-playing or something.

But she and Cormac were going to come face-to-face with a murderer. A guy who'd shown zero remorse after annihilating another human being. He was a psychopath with an army of people just like him, and she was going to saunter into his lion's den and offer him a free kill.

Teddy stole gulps of breath as she made her way to a quiet place outside the kitchen where she could think and hopefully calm her nerves.

She went directly for the mantle of the fireplace in the great room, gripping it, panic began to claw at her, seep into her bones, drag her deeper and deeper to its anxiety-riddled depths.

This would never work. Stas would catch them. Carmine would catch them trying to deceive him and she'd be dead. Cormac would be dead. They were all going to die!

A shiver beginning in her toes worked its way up to her arms, violently assaulting her, leaving her body one big tremble.

But then Cormac was there, slipping his arms around her and turning her into the shelter of his body. "Just breathe, Teddy."

She scrunched her eyes shut and gulped. "I shouldn't be like this. I don't know what's wrong with me. I'm a bounty hunter, for crap's sake! Why am I so scared?"

"Because you don't hunt to kill, honey. You hunt to capture. But I promise, I won't let anything happen to you. If anyone makes a wrong move, I've got your back."

Her heart began to crash hard against her ribs, panic-attack style. She'd had them after her last run-in with Dennis, she knew the signs. But now wasn't the time.

"Tell me about why you got in on the bounty hunting."

Her throat tightened, but telling Cormac her story helped her focus on something else. "Because of my dad. He was killed in a bar fight and the guy who did it was prosecuted and sent to jail, but he escaped. We were just kids when it happened initially, but when the guy got out, we were adults. My mom was gone by then, but we never forgot how hard life became because my dad was gone. How much she missed him, how much we all missed him. So we hunted the bastard. Tracked him and strung him up and brought him in for my father, who was the kindest man I've ever known. It was the beginning of what became a profitable business, for the most part. I learned from my brothers how to track when I was little. I got so much better at it than them, that now, whenever we get a bounty in the forest, I take it."

"Which was why I ended up darted," he chuckled, running his hands along her spine.

"If I make a million apologies, it'll never be enough."

"Nah. It'll be a great story to tell our grandchildren someday, don't you think? How Grammy and Paw-Paw met one cold winter day when Grammy was out huntin' men."

Teddy giggled against his flannel shirt, the tension in her back easing at the mention of a possible future.

"And Sanctuary? I never really got to ask you about it last night because, well, drugged, or whatever Arch did to us. Tell me about it. It's a wildlife rescue and rehabilitation, right?"

Her heart sank. He had no way of knowing the dire circumstances of her home away from home back in Colorado, but every bounty she took was because of the animals she loved so much. What would happen to Mr. Noodles, her deaf Macaque monkey, who was already angry and frustrated because he struggled with communication?

He'd end up sent to someone who didn't understand him and would lock him away from the other monkeys because he was volatile. But what he needed was understanding and integration.

And Suits, her Emperor penguin who'd been born with a deformed foot? Who'd help him acclimate to new surroundings? And the giraffes and the otters...

"Yes, Sanctuary rescues and rehabs all sorts of wildlife, and even an exotic or two. And it was where I worked. By the time I get back, I'd lay bets Sanctuary will have closed its doors. The bank is foreclosing on them," she said, her voice hitching. She should have been long done with her bounty by now and back with a nice bulk payment for the bank.

If things hadn't gone so wrong.

Her chest ached for the animals that were her heart. They knew her. She knew them. Every idiosyncrasy, every quirk, every special need. They'd never known anything but her and the staff at Sanctuary. There's nothing she'd miss more than her time with them.

"Where will all the animals go?"

"I don't know. The bank's in charge of that. I'm sick with worry over what'll happen to them—where they'll end up. Some of them are bonded and can't ever be let out of captivity because they won't survive. We tried to get the bank to appoint me their guardians, because I know each and every one of them and all of their needs. But they wouldn't allow it. Likely, they'll end up separated and shipped off to zoos around the country without the special care they need. I wanted to help. I thought this... Never mind. It's over, I guess."

"Hold up. Was the money from my bounty supposed to help save Sanctuary?"

She kept her face hidden. "Why would you think that?"

"I saw the price on my forehead on the news for information just leading to my arrest last night, Teddy. I imagine the bounty on me was pretty high, too. Were you going to use that money for Sanctuary?"

"Carmine made up the damn bounty on you. Falsified all sorts of databases. There *was* never any bounty for you..."

"Teddy. Just be straight with me. If we're going to do this, let's do it right. Honesty's right. So spit it out."

Her sigh was ragged. "Okay, yes. But it doesn't really matter anyway. They never wanted me to catch you. Just lead them to you. They would have killed me once they got you and the bounty deposit wouldn't matter anyway. It was lose-lose to begin with."

She felt his chest expand beneath her cheek. "Damn these bastards. Damn them. Listen, when this is done, I'll help you with Sanctuary, okay? We'll figure something else out."

"You're very sweet to offer, but you don't know thing one about wildlife rehabilitation, and the kind of dedication it takes to save some of these animals is stressful at the best of times. You have to really love animals, carry around a pager and a cell phone, sometimes two. You get involved.

You suffer with them. You cry when there's nothing you can do but watch them die."

"Then we'll be stressed together. And it can't be all stressful. You've had success stories. I'm sure of it."

A tear slipped from her eye and rolled down her cheek. "How can you possibly know something like that?"

His chin dropped to the top of her head, resting there. "Because the Teddy I'm discovering is made of sheer grit and determination. You survived domestic violence and you're still standing. Taking bounties to help a place you love working for, even though I'm sure going back to bounty hunting was hard. Shit like what Dennis did to you can get in your head and ruin you. But you didn't let it. That, in and of itself, is a success."

Now her throat was so tight, she almost couldn't speak. "You'd come back to Colorado?"

"Once this was over, I never planned on going anywhere else. I love Colorado—despite the fact that it was my prison. There's nothing left for me here. Toni's in this other realm and getting ready to marry a prince from another time and place, and my house...well, I imagine it's long gone by now. The bank only goes so long without a payment."

"I'm sorry, Cormac. God, they've ruined your life." When she reflected on all he'd lost, she had no right to complain.

"Not all of it. If not for them, I wouldn't have met you. So let's make a pact, okay. Right here, right now."

"Okay. Pact me."

"When this is over, let's get on a plane to Colorado and get you back home to the animals you love and your brothers, who are probably gonna want to kick my half-breed ass. Let's figure out a way to save Sanctuary, and in the process, let's get to know each other. I can't deny anymore that I feel something for you. I'm not even going to try. I'm about as attracted to you as anyone's ever been. I think you're sexy and smart, funny and kind. But you have faults. So do I. I'm stubborn and sarcastic when cornered. I'm not a morning person. In fact, I'm normally a shithead in my first waking hour. I've just been hiding it because I'm a guest in someone else's house. I'm a lot of things. But we've known each other all of three days and under some pretty messed-up circumstances. I want to see all sides of you, and I want you to see all the sides of me. Good, bad, and even ugly."

Her eyes closed as she listened to the steady rhythm of his heart. "So what are you asking?"

"I want to use these feelings I'm having for you as a building block to a solid foundation for us. I want your trust. I want your honesty. I want to learn all the things that make Teddy who she is. I want the time to do that, and I especially don't want you to feel rushed."

"So what you're saying is we do this the right way? Courtship, dating, texting, flowers—"

"Flowers? Are you a flower kind of girl?"

"What if I am?"

"I thought you were more of a weapons-and-ammo chick."

Teddy laughed, all her fears set aside for the moment until she remembered what they were about to do. "I'm petrified."

Cormac held her tighter, dropping a kiss on the top of her head. "This should be the part where I tell you I'm not. To reassure you—be all big and strong—but I am, too. I'm petrified you'll get hurt, and I'm man enough to admit it. Going in with some fear is a good thing. It means we'll be cautious. But I *need* you to be careful, Teddy. Do everything as we planned. Follow the script, because I'm pretty sure I couldn't handle one more person taken from me—especially not you."

"I'm gonna try like hell to do this right, I promise. I don't want you to be cheated out of buying me guns and ammo. Oh, and camouflage. I love camouflage."

Just as Cormac barked a laugh, Nina poked her head around the corner of the great room with Marty right behind her, fiddling with the red wig she'd secured to her head. "Saddle up, girls. Tonight, we ride!"

Squaring her shoulders, Teddy tried to focus on all the things Cormac had said—especially the part about having a future where they would really get to know one another.

It beat the alternative.

Which was dead.

Chapter 14

"Who the hell is this?" the heavily accented Russian voice, deep and thick, growled into her ear.

Nina gripped her hand as Teddy clung to the burner cell and Carl sat at her feet, letting his head rest on her knee.

Be confidant, Teddy Bear. You've got what they want.

"I think you know exactly who this is."

Yeah. Grrrr, you cold-blooded killer!

Nina gave her the thumbs up while Cormac smoothed his hand over her back.

"Tell me, *malutka*, what can Stas do for you this snowy evening?"

She licked her lips and closed her eyes. "I have what you want."

"And what do I want, Poopsie?" he drawled, clearly amused.

She imagined him sitting behind some long, shiny black desk with sexily-clad women draped on his arm, a cigar dangling from the corner of his mouth, surrounded by burgundy drapes on tall windows and leather furniture as he laughingly considered her words while he stroked his exotic Bengal tiger.

That rather burned her britches. So she dropped the bomb in his lap. "Cormac and Toni Vitali."

There was a pause, a stomach-turning, nerve-racking pause, and then he laughed, a deep, gurgling belly laugh before he barked out a demand. "Speak!"

"Meet me at Leningrad's Vodka Bar—one hour. I'll have them with me. I trade them for my freedom from you."

"And how do I know you speak the truth, *malutka*? What proof do you have that my sweet Antonia is with you?"

Not a question that was in the script. Shit! "You'll just have to trust me," she countered with alarming confidence that surprised even her, her heart punching the inside of her chest. "And it has to be you or *no one*. I'm not meeting with one of your flunkeys. If you're not there, no deal."

She held her breath while she waited for his answer. Seconds ticked by— seconds that felt like hours.

"*Dah*. You come. You bring my precious Antonia and her brother. We'll drink to old friends."

And then the line went dead. Just like that, she had exactly one hour before the universe decided if she and Cormac would see another day.

* * *

Cormac sat in the back of the black SUV Nina drove through the sleet and snow like she'd been possessed by Dale Earnhardt Jr. and willed his thoughts to the task at hand. Forced himself to stop letting his imagination get the better of him, to stop letting endless scenarios of doom play out in his mind and just focus.

Get himself and Teddy out from under Stas's thumb and get the evidence they needed to put the son of a bitch and his buddies in jail. Oh, and maybe knock the shit out of Andre for biting him.

Teddy sat in silence beside him, her jaw clenched, her eyes glazed, her hand cold and clammy.

As they turned into the side street a block away from Stas's favorite hangout and Nina pulled to an abrupt stop, he grabbed Teddy's hand, pulling her to him. "You do exactly as you were told. Just like we rehearsed it, you hear me? If one thing goes wrong, get the hell out, Teddy. *Get out.* Don't think about me and what could happen—just get to Nina and Arch."

She nodded, her breathing shallow and rapid.

"Be safe, okay? Don't let him get to you. No matter what he says or does, stick to the plan."

"You, too," she whispered, gripping the front of his sweatshirt.

He pressed a hard kiss to her mouth before letting her go. The dome light in the car clicked on as Marty opened the door and hopped out, her heel—heels Toni would have worn—landing on the snowy sidewalk.

Arch turned around then, his fedora jauntily covering one eye. "When you are through with this ruffian, we shall celebrate, Teddy Bear. Hot toddies for all."

Teddy gave him a wisp of a smile and nodded, squeezing his weathered hand.

Nina looked into the rearview mirror and winked. "Kick some fucking Russian ass. You got this, kiddo." Then she looked to Cormac and nodded. "You watch my girl in there, Pooh Bear. Don't go gettin' your ass shot."

He gripped her shoulder briefly and nodded. "Will do. Be safe. Lay low."

Nina rolled down the window and looked directly at Marty. "Remember your fat ass is stuffed into that tight dress like some kinda sausage and you have to make time allowances for your getaway, Blondie."

Marty's eyes narrowed as she bumped fists with her bestie. "Fuck off, Ex-Elvira. And I'd better not see your face inside that bar, or I'm gonna turn your intestines into wall art. Now put your hands on the wheel at ten and two and do your job, chauffer."

Nina snapped her teeth at her friend and rolled the window back up, driving away, leaving just the three of them on the sidewalk under the streetlamp.

Snow battered their faces; sleet slicked their clothing, giving a glossy sheen to Marty's dress.

Are we ready?" Teddy asked, her voice shaky and shuddering.

Both Marty and Cormac turned around, putting their hands behind their backs.

As the cold plastic of the zip tie tightened around his wrists, and the butt of a pistol pressed between his shoulder blades, he sucked in a breath and sent up a silent prayer.

Just keep Teddy safe.

Whatever it takes, keep her safe.

* * *

Loud folk music blared from the interior of the shadowy bar when they first entered, smoke filled the long, wide room and the scent of vodka, strong and Russian-made, permeated her nose.

Her hand shook momentarily, but she gripped the handle of the gun harder to steady herself, finding Darnell in the tiny, dark corner of the bar and using him as her center.

The moment they entered, he slipped his bulky body down along the plastic material of the booth like a melting puddle of wax, and huddled under the table.

Okay, step one complete.

Step two. Making an entrance.

Speaking of, their entrance was anything but dramatic. In her mind, she'd imagined the moment they stepped foot into the smoky, dark, red and purple room, guns would cock to the tune of Clint Eastwood's infamous *Dirty Harry*.

Instead, four or five rough-looking men good-naturedly drank from glass tumblers at a long stretch of bar, laughed and chatted in Russian, and in general didn't even realize they'd entered at all.

Which might have been a bit of a downer, but instead gave her too much time to think about what she was supposed to say next.

Marty wiggled her fingers, brushing the hem of Teddy's vest. "Psst. It's your turn, honey. Just like we rehearsed, remember?" she whispered out of the side of her mouth.

But she couldn't remember. She was drawing a blank. Oh. God.

"Teddy!" Cormac whisper-yelled. "Demand to see Stas. Remember? You say, 'Where's Stas Vasilyev?'"

Oh right. Step two.

She cleared her throat as the music continued to play and no one paid any mind to them. "Hey!" she shouted, sort of. "Where's Stas Vasilyev?"

Nothing. Not a soul turned from the bar.

"Louder, honey," Marty prompted. "Then remember, when they respond, shove us to the corner of the bar where those booths are so we're in the shadows and they can't see my face."

Fear and panic began that nauseating roll in her stomach again, and coupled with the frustration of being completely ignored, was probably what made her finally get some steam.

"Heeeeyyyy!" she roared, using her best bear's voice.

Everything stopped then. The music, the bartender pouring drinks, the five thugs sitting at the bar.

Well. She smiled in satisfaction. That was more like it.

"Push us into the booth, Teddy. Do it like you mean it," Cormac uttered under his breath.

Oh yeah. There was the opening line and then there was the shoving part. Darnell had come earlier in the day to scope the layout of the bar so they knew exactly how and where to position Marty in order to keep her in the shadows and not reveal her face, to make Stas think she was Toni.

So get everyone's attention, shove, demand to see Stas. Okay. Got it.

With all her strength, she knocked Marty and Cormac sideways to the tune of Marty's yelp and Cormac's grunt. But then there was a loud clatter as Marty crashed into a table that wasn't supposed to be next to the booth and fell over it with no way to brace herself from the fall.

Her legs flew up in the air and she lost one of her heels, but by God, her wig stayed securely on her head.

Teddy was quick to react, but Marty gave a curt shake of her head to stop her from helping her from the floor before she curled into a ball, keeping her face hidden.

Oh damn. *Think, Teddy. Think!*

"Stop being so damn rough with her!" Cormac shouted at her from the floor, his voice dripping with distress, his eyes prompting her to react and remember what their roles were.

She was handing them over to save her own hide and they were her ticket to getting the hell away from Carmine, the cops, and Stas. Act accordingly. Be cagey, nervous, but above all, be angry. *Marty and Cormac are your hostages,* Wanda had coached. *You fought long and hard to get them and you're livid they've involved you in this and put your life in danger. Behave as such.*

Right. Angry.

Wow. Cormac had conveyed all that information with his eyes. He was good.

But oh, Jesus, this meant improv—something that was not in the script.

Gathering her wits, Teddy waved the gun at them and made a scary face. "Get in the damn booth and shut up!"

Marty winked just as she scrambled into the booth, pretending to cower behind Cormac, whose shoulders were wide enough to keep her face covered.

"Don't move or I'll blow your heads off!" she shouted from clenched teeth.

Cormac mouthed the word "overkill."

Okay, too much. Next task. Stas. She had to demand to see Stas, and do it without her voice trembling in fear. "Where is Stas Vasilyev? Tell him to get his ass out here now. I have something for him!"

From the far end of the bar, a colorfully beaded curtain parted and a man, an enormous, bulky, gorgeous man, who pushed his way through almost in slow motion, appeared. The beads clacked together, falling against his long, lean body before revealing him totally.

Tall and darkly European, he wore tight jeans, a black knit sweater and a red scarf around his neck. His eyes were dark and smolderingly sexy, his nose straight, giving him a chiseled look, his mouth full and kissable. His hand was around one of the glass tumblers, his pinky extended as he rolled the clear liquid and took a long gulp.

He reminded Teddy of one of those artists, tortured and plagued by his creative genius.

Then he smiled and strolled toward her with the kind of confidence only a psychopath possessed.

Her hands began to shake.

There was supposed to be another step here. She just couldn't remember what the hell it was.

"Ah, *malutka*. Welcome!" he said jovially, as though he were hosting a Tupperware party. "Come! Drink with me!" He slapped his hand on the shiny bar as he sat on the barstool, and instantly a bartender appeared with a glass holding what she assumed was vodka.

Stepfourstepfourstepfour—what the hell was step four? Was she even on step four? Maybe she was on five?

Wait. She remembered. No booze. Don't let Stas take you off course. Stick to the plan.

"I'm not thirsty," she croaked. "I came here to make a deal."

He cocked his dark head, his ponytail sleek and sultry, his bedroom eyes calling to her. Well, she could certainly see how Toni had fallen for him. He really was pretty hot.

Hot and a psychopath, Teddy Bear. Nutball alert—do not sympathize with the bounty.

Stas gave her his best wounded look, but then he grinned. "A deal? I like pretty girls who like to make deals. Why don't you put the gun down and we talk. We are civilized people, yes?"

Step whatever the number was—tell him the deal. Present the deal.

Licking her lips, Teddy gripped the gun even harder. "Not a chance. I brought my part of the bargain, now you have to give me something in return or I blow your head off."

Was it blow your head off or blow your balls off? She couldn't remember that part very well because Nina had been so busy naming body parts, she lost track.

Stas's head fell back on his shoulders when he laughed, revealing the deep olive tone to his skin. As he laughed, so did his goons. Because that's what goons did. When the boss mock-laughed, you joined in.

She caught sight of Andre, the slimy, smelly prick who'd jammed a knife in her gut, and fought the impulse to rush him and knock his disgusting ass off the barstool.

Stas popped his lips and batted his eyelashes. "Tell me, my *krasavitsa*, what can Stas do for you? You say all these threats, but you do not say what is on your mind. Get to it. I'm a very busy man."

Step six. Make him admit he's a murderer.

Teddy gulped, running her tongue over her dry lower lip. "You can leave me the hell alone! I had nothing to do with any of this. That dirty cop Carmine sent me on a wild goose chase to help him clean up *his* mess, the incompetent jackhole, because he was too stupid to figure out where Vitali was on his own."

Someone burst from the shadows with a hiss of rage. "I'll kill you, you fucking bitch!"

Enter Carmine. Perfect. Two birds, one stone. She hadn't expected him to be here, but she was prepared for him to show up. This *was* in the script.

Teddy waved the gun at him, her hands no longer shaking. Rather, she wanted to rip his face from his body. "Like when you tried to take me out on the Island? Back off, chicken-shit!" she screamed, spit flying from her mouth. "Or I'll blow your head off, too! You used me to find the man you wanted to kill and then you came gunning for me. First you tried to kill me, which you blew sky-high, you bumbling idiot, then you broadcast my face all over the news to smoke me out because you're too stupid to come and get me yourself, you big tattletale!"

Tattletale? Good use of forceful adjectives, Teddy Bear.

Stas was on his feet in an instant, grabbing Carmine and hurling him to the ground. He rammed his heel into his chest and pinned him to the floor. "Were you a mean boy to my *malutka?*" he taunted down at Carmine.

Teddy didn't give Carmine the chance to answer. "You know damn well what he did to me! He set me up!" she shouted.

"Tut-tut, dirty cop," Stas chided Carmine, using the toe of his pointed boot. And then he called out another order over his shoulder. "Check her."

Three of the men were up on their feet in no time flat, but she was prepared for this. They wanted to see if she had some kind of recording device on her before Stas spoke to her.

Teddy whipped the gun upward and pointed it at Andre's ugly mug. "Not him! He's the asshole who rammed a knife in my gut because he was too much of a dick to take a beating from a woman. And his breath smells like toxic waste."

The men all began to howl with laughter, jamming their fists into Andre's ribs and razzing him while he scowled.

Stas snapped his fingers, eliminating all sound. He swished a finger at the biggest of the lot. "Bogdan. You. Go."

Bogdan approached her with caution, his youthful face leery until she held her arms up. "If you go anywhere you shouldn't on my body, I splatter your face all over this bar."

Cormac coughed, likely reminding her she was taking her method acting too far.

As he patted her down, Stas eyed her, his gaze never straying from her face. When Bogdan nodded to show she was clean, he approached, totally unaffected by the gun in her hand.

He stood toe to toe with her, his arms crossed over his chest, oozing charm and sniffing the air around her. "You are like us?"

Teddy moved the gun between them and sniffed back. She couldn't tell what breed he was, but he *was* bear shifter, just as she'd thought. With that, she prayed he hadn't scented Marty or Cormac. Nina had covered them in something that was supposed to disguise their scents. The last thing they wanted was for Stas to discover Cormac and Marty were worthy opponents.

There was no use denying what she was, so Teddy gave him a curt nod. "I am. Coincidence, right?"

His eyebrow rose upward. "So what is it you want in return from Stas, eh? Tell me details, *malutka*."

Now that he was this close, her heart began to clang in her chest again. But she barreled ahead into step seven.

Close the deal.

"I want you to let me go, free and clear. I had nothing to do with any of this. Your goon dragged me into it by setting me up with his bullshit bounty story. You should be paying me for finding this douchebag Vitali for you. I didn't even know you existed until all this went down. I've heard the whole story about how you killed some guy, who I bet was chicken-shit's partner, Mauricio, and Vitali's sister saw you, then you kidnapped her and her brother, blah-blah-blah. But here's the thing. I don't care! I just want to get the hell away from you *and* them, and I want your assurance you'll leave me alone. Have Carmine fix what he did by plastering my face all over the news and let me go. *Forever.*"

Stas looked at her a long time, the wheels of his mind turning with diabolic plots, no doubt. Then suddenly his face was wreathed in a wide smile, lighting up when his gaze strayed to the corner of the room where Cormac and Marty sat.

"Of course! How could I forget about my Antonia? It's been so long since we saw each other. Where have you been? Come to me, my dove," he said, holding out his hand.

Cue Cormac and his acting debut.

He shielded Marty from Stas, keeping her body behind him. "You leave her the fuck alone, Vasilyev!"

Stas sighed as though bored, his shoulders sagging as he turned to face Cormac. "*You*," he said with a freakishly fond look of pride in his eyes and a stab in the air of his index finger. "You are strong, like bull. No crying or whining the whole time we keep you in cellar. We chop your finger off and you hardly make sound. Brave boy, *dah?*"

"You son of a bitch, you didn't just hack off my finger. You ruined my goddamn life!"

164

"*What?*" He gave Cormac a look of utter astonishment. "You don't like Colorado? It is much like my home. Beautiful snow, animals everywhere. I did you favor!"

"You killed a man, held me hostage, and I had to hide like the criminal. How the fuck is that doing me a favor?"

Stas clucked his tongue and stroked the fringe on his red scarf. "Your sister, she talks too much. Just like woman, yes? Always with the gab-gab-gab. It's a pity she must die. She is so pretty. Pretty girls should live forever."

Marty whimpered; for effect or as a signal, Teddy couldn't be sure. One thing she *could* be sure of, Cormac wasn't acting. His rage, pent up for so long, was seeping out.

But Stas still hadn't admitted to killing Carmine's partner.

Stas made a move toward Cormac and Marty, but Teddy waved him away with the gun. "I didn't hear you say we had a deal. Them in exchange for my freedom."

"Shh, shh, shh, Poopsie. I'm thinking." He tapped a finger to the side of his head.

"Don't do it, Stas! Don't let the bitch go or you'll regret it!" Carmine yelled, scrambling up from the floor, his round face beet red. "She'll run right to the cops. No loose ends, Stas. We fucking agreed!"

Teddy gritted her teeth and held up the gun, wanting nothing more than to shoot Carmine's eyeballs out. All her anger, all her helplessness over the situation with Dennis rose like a hot air balloon and exploded inside her, taking her by surprise.

She didn't know where it came from. She didn't know why she wasn't able to contain it, but she was mad as hell, and she wasn't acting any longer when she belted out, "Shut up, you mealy-mouthed partner killer! You killed your partner because he found out about Stas greasing your palms, didn't he?"

Carmine's face became a mask of fury as he shuffled from foot to foot. "Fuck you, you dumb cunt!"

Teddy lifted the gun higher, aiming between his eyes with no interference from Stas. "That's what you did, didn't you, you prick! He found out what you were doing at that car dealership. He caught you sticking your hand in the pot, and then you and your filthy friend Andre took him out with Stas's approval because he was going to fuck you right up the ass, wasn't he? He'd ruin your career, your wife and children would have to hide in shame. And then you covered it all up, you coward! How'd you do it, Cop Killer?" she seethed. "Did you whisper in someone's ear at the department, tell them maybe Mauricio was unstable? Or did you drop hints he might have disappeared because he was unsavory? You stupid bitch. You're just someone's little paid *bitch*!"

Carmine shook with anger, every vein in his neck bulging, his bloodshot eyes blasting arrows of pure hatred her way. "He was gonna goddamn snitch! I tried to do him a favor by bringin' him into the mix. His kid gettin' ready to go off to college was killin' him on a cop's salary. He needed the fucking money! I told him I could help. I gave Stas my word Mauricio was good for it. But he fucking blew it. He fucking blew it all with his whining about truth and justice! So I took him out. Yeah, I did! It happened so fast, he didn't know what hit his snitch ass!"

Teddy fought to keep her horror on the inside, to keep from visibly shaking.

Stas sighed as though bored with the retelling of old kills. "It is true, *malutka*. He took my gun right from the waist of my jeans and pow-pow." He made a pretend gun of his thumb and forefinger and aimed it at Carmine. "We were all very surprised with our Carmine's behavior. He is, as you say, a dirty cop killer."

"On *his* order! I did it because he told me to do it! He's the one who told me to find Vitali, too. He said find Vitali or die!" Carmine wailed. "Don't know why the fuck he had Andre follow me when I damn well had it covered."

Stas scoffed his disapproval of Carmine. "Trust, you idiot! I cannot trust that you will do as you say! You are useless!"

Carmine hitched his jaw in fake Toni's direction before his desperate gaze fell back on Stas. "This all started with you and your nosy girlfriend!" he screeched. "Damn shame that bitch showed up at the dealership right after I got the fuck out of there or I'da killed her right then, too. No loose ends!"

Pretend like you don't care. Pretend like you don't care.

Teddy squared her shoulders. "I don't give a shit who you killed, you fucking baby! I'm warning you, stay the hell out of my damn way! If you don't agree to this, too, I'll shoot your damn dick off!"

"*Fuck youuu!*" he screamed, spit flying from between his thick lips.

"*Enough!*" Stas bellowed the order, his eyes like granite. Then he snapped his fingers and Bogdan was by his side again. He flicked his hand at Carmine. "Take him elsewhere. *Now.*"

Her chest heaved and her heart crashed against her ribs as she tried to catch her breath. But Stas wasn't done taunting her.

"Ahhh, my *malutka.* You are so feisty. If I had more time, I would take you to my apartment. We would share vodka, maybe a kiss or two…a cuddle, yes?"

Teddy kept her eye on the prize, refusing to allow him to egg her on. "Do we have a deal or not? I give you the Vitalis, give you my word I'll never rat on you about that bitch's partner, and you let me split free and clear. Deal?"

Just as Stas opened his mouth to answer, someone else burst through the door of the bar, taking everyone by surprise—even Stas's goons.

Teddy didn't have time to turn around before a large hand had wrapped itself around her hair and yanked her backward, making her lose her grip on the gun.

Her gun fell to the floor, skidding across the sticky surface until it hit something she couldn't see for the tight hold this person had on her hair.

Stas's thugs, though sluggish to react, were up and at the ready, their guns cocked, their war faces on.

Teddy reached upward to try to get away, but that was when she felt the barrel end of a gun jammed between her shoulder blades.

And then a very familiar voice spoke, a haunting nightmare from her past.

"Hi, honey! I'm home!" her ex-husband, Dennis, crooned in her ear.

Chapter 15

Her stomach sank to the floor as Dennis began to drag her toward the door, but Stas had apparently taken a shine to her, because he thundered, "Don't move, or I have my boys shoot you between the eyes!"

Dennis stopped cold, his breathing huffing from his chest.

"Bet you didn't think we'd ever see each other again, huh, Teddy Bear," he hissed in her ear to the tune of Cormac's low growl.

"How did you find me?"

Jesus. What kind of stupid question is that? Who gave a shit how he found you? He found you!

Dennis cackled, nipping her earlobe. "Aw, Lovebug. You know how resourceful I am. I broke into the ranch and it was just my luck, Viktor and Vadim had written down your buddy Nina's address. It was right there on the counter! Imagine my surprise when I saw you were in New York. I couldn't believe it. You hate the city. So I borrowed Daddy's plane and here I am. I watched. I waited while you were in that castle. A *castle*—crazy, right? Anyway, I knew you'd come out of there at some point and when you did, I followed you. Easy-peasy. And now here we are. Reunited." He yanked her hair, sending a violent shiver down her spine.

Teddy held her breath as Stas approached.

He sucked his cheeks inward. "This is all very nice, but I am busy man. Now, where are you taking my *malutka?*"

Teddy felt Dennis tense behind her, tightening his grip on her by wrapping his arm around her neck and squeezing. "Stay the fuck where you are and no one gets hurt," he ordered.

Stas's chin lifted in indignation and his eyes narrowed dangerously. "Do you know who I am?"

"I don't give a shit!" Dennis sneered. "This bitch is mine. Now back the fuck off, tell your shitheads to back the fuck off, and shut the fuck up, and we'll leave here all nice and peaceful. I've waited a goddamn long time to get my hands on my wife. This is between her and me. Now I said, back off!"

"Oh dear," Stas muttered and clucked his tongue in that condescending way he had, then made pleading eyes at Teddy. "You did not tell Stas you were married, *malutka*. This hurts me so. I thought we were beginning a beautiful friendship, but you start our journey by deceiving me?"

Her neck ached as she struggled against Dennis's steel grip. "Dennis isn't my husband anymore!" she managed to squeak out around the pressure constricting her throat.

Stas stood up straight and eyed them critically. "Then it would appear we have a standoff. I will not let you take my sweet bird, and you do not wish to give her back to me. Whatever shall we do, *Dennis?*"

Her knees trembled. The last time Dennis had her in his clutches, he'd almost killed her, and now she had not one but two psychopaths fighting over her. She had to do something, but fear paralyzed her, rooted her to the spot as Dennis's breath rasped against her ear, his heavy breathing making her cringe.

"Who is this guy? Is he your boyfriend?" Dennis spat, shoving the gun into her flesh again.

The sharp zing of pain made her arch away from him. "Dennis, let me go! You have no idea who you're dealing with!" she shrieked, unable to contain her fear.

If nothing else, Dennis was the lesser of two evils, but with all these guns pointed at her, there was nowhere to go and she wasn't leaving this room without Cormac and fake Toni.

"Tell me, Dennis," Stas crowed. "Are you going to kill my pretty bird? What could someone so pretty have done to you?"

Teddy's heart stopped. Yep. He was probably going to take her out. Finish the job he'd begun over a year ago, and she was helpless to stop him.

"It's none of your business!" he screamed, his voice rising, his movements jerky and stuttered.

Teddy knew that tone. She knew it meant he was on the verge of cracking. He'd sounded exactly like this the moment before he'd pushed her over that ravine. When he realized she was never coming back to their marriage, he'd lost his mind, and he was going to lose it again.

She had to do something.

What? What could she possibly do without creating all-out havoc for everyone else?

Stas shook his head and put his hands on his hips. "You do know you will never get out the door alive, don't you, foolish boy?"

And that's when it hit her—Stas had nothing to lose. If Dennis dragged her out the door and his band of merry men took shots at them, Stas's problems were solved. She'd be dead and then he'd kill Cormac and Marty. Game over.

Her guts tied all up in a knot. Her heart pulsed in her ears as the stench of Dennis's indecision and sweat permeated her nose.

What to do, what to do? Teddy's panic level rose by at least five hundred notches, but circumstances kept her from making a choice.

The choice was made for her when the rectangular window of the bar, facing the street, blew wide open, shattering glass everywhere, spraying the shards across the room.

Wanda came tumbling in like some freakish gymnast on steroids, nailing her landing and making it stick, before she ran after Andre, grabbing him by the neck.

Bullets began to fly in all directions from Stas's men, whizzing around the air like deadly flies, all aimed at Wanda.

That was when Cormac burst from the booth, his mouth wide open as he roared his rage. His neck bulged, his fists still behind his back, but he broke the restraints without missing a beat.

Oh God. He was going to shift. He was upset and angry and those emotions had fueled a shift.

She had to stop him or risk his being discovered by people passing by.

"No, Cormac! No!" she screamed while bullets flew. She attempted to free herself from Dennis, but he was too damn strong.

Dennis howled before he threw her to the ground with such force, she was sure she was going to have another cracked rib.

Which made her mad as hell. Goddamn it, hadn't she been knocked around enough? What the fuck was with the manhandling her these days? Every time she turned around, someone was kicking her ass, and she'd had enough.

But the outraged roar from Cormac set her into motion. His bones crunched, shifted, twisted until he was forced forward to his haunches, almost knocking what was left of his human chin on the ground.

"Cormac, no!" she screamed once more, but he was too far gone and as he fully shifted. His deep black coat shimmering under the bar lights, he headed straight for Dennis, his gaze deadlocked.

She caught the surprise in Stas's eyes when Cormac took shape, no longer cool and unruffled, and clearly shocked that Cormac was now one of them. He'd been smart to keep that hidden for as long as he had while he was huddled in the booth.

He was impressive in bear shift, enormous, wide, solid, a deep almost ebony. His coat was healthy and shiny, his paws easily ten inches wide, his hump, the muscle between their shoulder blades they used to dig, was mammoth.

But he'd never withstand a beating from seasoned vets like Andre and Stas.

They'd kill him. If she was sure of nothing else, she was sure, in comparison to bears who'd shifted all their lives, Cormac was weak.

Dennis, who had no time to react and shift himself, began to shoot in wild arcs.

Marty, who'd shifted now, too, howled, long and eerily pitched, the sound whipping around the room and hitting Teddy's eardrums at every angle. Marty lunged for Dennis, successfully knocking the gun out of his hand, but she crashed into the side of the bar, taking some stools and a man or two with her. The impact left her unmoving on the floor.

And that was when it turned into werewolf versus bear.

Howls roared through the bar, making it quake as the shift took over Stas's men. The floor crunching beneath bear paws to the tune of broken glass.

Cormac changed direction and stalked two of Stas's men, tearing after them with a loud roar.

Carmine Ragusi, weenie that he was, came around the corner, witnessed the rampage, and huddled in a ball, sliding down the wall, his eyes wide, his stout body quivering.

Andre shifted right in Wanda's clutches, his clothes blowing off his body and his teeth, sharp and gleaming, sprouting forth in the low light of the bar.

He went for Wanda's neck, but she managed to hold him off by grabbing his snout and flipping him to the ground, breaking one of the cocktail tables, the wood splintering and flying.

And then she shifted, too, with a piercing wail full of anger. She went for Andre like a rabid animal, rushing him as he reared upward before falling on his back and crushing a portion of the bar.

Darnell bellowed from under the table where he'd hidden earlier, "Teddy! Look out!"

Teddy scrambled on the floor, turning just in time to see Dennis racing toward her, his eyes wild with a year's worth of hatred. As his legs pumped, he began to melt, his clothes falling away, his body distorting until he, too, was in bear shift. His enormous head loomed closer and closer. The sound of his paws pounding on the floor, over glass, over bodies scattered from one end of the big room to the other, resonated in her ears.

In that moment, that paralyzing, heart-pounding moment, she froze.

He was going to kill her. He'd win. He'd succeed in finishing what he'd started.

All the ugly words and cruel jaunts raced through her mind. A year's worth of healing and fighting her way back into shape would be for nothing.

She was nothing. He'd said she was nothing. A no one. And now, he'd win.

Helplessness swarmed her, invaded her, took hold of her, shaking her to her core.

You're nothing, Teddy!

No! Nonono!

Anger welled, rising up, shoving its way through all the ugly words, the cruel taunts, and a surge of anguish catapulted her to shift. Rage fueled her rapid change, her bones jolted, cracked, realigned—and then she roared.

A roar of raw fury, an ear-shattering screech of a declaration.

This was motherfucking war.

Darnell began to lob fireballs just as Teddy rose on her hind legs and Dennis barreled toward her. Smoke filled the room, the plastic curtain melted, sending up a rancid stench. Darnell caught Dennis in the hide, but it was as if he was unaware his fur was burning because Dennis kept coming at her.

Matching his growl, Teddy charged, falling to all fours, rooting her paws into the ground with each stride.

She headed straight for him everything else around her blurred. The bullets, the screams of fear, pain. The scent of blood. All of it faded and it was just she and Dennis.

They crashed into each other, the power of his bulky body pounding into hers, stealing the breath from her lungs.

They fell to the ground, hundreds of pounds slamming to the floor, and then she was on top of him, victorious, heady with her coup.

He struggled, bellowing his surprise and outrage, twisting his bulk to attempt to escape.

But Teddy lifted her front paw high in the air, ready to swipe at his throat, prepared to wipe his useless ass from the face of the planet—and then she heard Stas, far off and almost distant, leaving her surprised he hadn't shifted, too. His voice clear, his words succinct and deadly.

"Kill them!" Stas hollered the order to the two men left standing. But Wanda went for them, with Darnell hot on her heels. Wanda's jaws opened wide as she made a dive for Bogdan, flattening him against the wall before they both crashed to the ground.

From out of nowhere, Andre charged her Teddy, his fierce growl ringing out, reverberating in the fiery bar as he knocked her from Dennis, leaving Teddy crumpled in the corner.

The pictures on the wall fell, cracking her on the head, splintered wood frames, aglow with flames, falling in her eyes.

While Teddy fought to clear her vision and regain her bearings, a howl from Marty sang out as she leapt from one end of the bar, aimed right for Andre.

So many things happened at once then. Just as Teddy was regaining her footing, Stas appeared beside Andre, gun in hand as Marty in wolf form flew in a graceful arc, slicing the air.

Teddy glimpsed Nina at the smashed window, snow blowing around her dark beauty, her eyes assessing what was about to happen in less than a second.

Stas had the gun pointed at Marty; he was going to shoot.

Nina's long limbs and dark hair flashed in Teddy's line of vision, her body launching forward from the gaping hole in the window directly in front of Stas.

She bellowed in an anguished cry of battle, "Not on my watch, motherfucker!"

Just before Stas fired his gun—the blast ripping through the sounds of grunts and howls.

In that split-second, that horrible, terrifying second, Teddy saw Nina's face. Beautiful, full of anguish, fear riddling her deep dark eyes, before she went limp from the impact of the bullet.

Marty was in danger, and Nina had protected her. Just like always. Just like all the stories she'd listen to them laugh over while they'd made dinner and played board games. Not heeding the words of her friends, throwing herself without thought into the line of fire. Because Marty was her friend.

Nina crumpled to the ground, an ugly crimson splotch spreading where her heart beat.

Marty's head reared back, her mournful cry filled with sorrow.

And that was when Teddy recovered her mojo.

No one was supposed to die. These people weren't supposed to sacrifice themselves in her stead. The plan had been so simple. Get in. Get Stas's confession on record, call the cops. Go home.

But nothing had gone as planned, and even if it meant doing life, Teddy wanted someone to die. She wanted everyone who'd hurt Cormac and these people she admired to die.

She wanted it to hurt. Hurt so bad they prayed for death.

With that one mission in mind, Teddy saw red, a red haze of an agonizing death, washing over Stas and the last of his still-standing goons and Dennis.

That was when she reared up and ran, head down, eyes glazed, straight at Dennis and Stas.

She heard nothing, saw nothing but the end goal.

Yet, even as she launched herself at them, Dennis was gearing up, too, and he sprang into action alongside Stas, who shifted where he stood. Powerful and wicked with rage, Stas rocketed into an all-out assault.

The pair of them coming at her, all thick muscle and fur, didn't daunt her even a little. The moment had come to wipe the earth of their scourge.

Teddy roared one last time, her final wail of fury, before she set her sights on ramming into them.

Stas's teeth were barred, ready to sink into her flesh. Dennis, too, had widened his mouth, his yellowed chops dripping his special brand of angry venom.

And then she stumbled, lost her footing on someone's gun.

A fireball screamed through the air, disorienting her, and Stas and Dennis took that opportunity to pounce.

The force of their weight blew her into the wall, sheetrock crumbling around her.

This was it. The moment men like Stas and Dennis won. She knew it. She was prepared for it even as she vowed to struggle to her death.

Until there was another shriek, deep and heated, shaking the entire room.

Cormac's bulky body shot forward, and with his head down, he crashed into Stas and Dennis, knocking them clear across the room and almost over the bar

He didn't stop to catch his breath. No, he rushed them, didn't give them the chance to regain their footing before he was on Dennis's back and Wanda was on Stas.

Dennis rolled and went for Cormac's throat with a screech of torment, his jaws but a half-inch from the meaty flesh. However, Cormac was too quick. He raised his paw high in the air and took a long swipe.

 The tear of flesh made a sickening ripping noise, blood spurting from Dennis's throat in gushes of thick red as he went limp.

Cormac huffed, his broad chest heaving, his nostrils flaring before he let his head fall between his shoulders and his shift began to take hold.

Wanda held Stas on the ground, her body realizing its human shape once again.

Arch was there just as sirens rang out in the distance, throwing clothes at Wanda and Marty, who crawled to where Nina lie, her sobs cutting through the wail of the police cars Arch and Nina had been told to call if they were in the bar too long.

Carl appeared, his greenish-pale face a mask of pain. But he handed clothes to Cormac and Teddy so they could dress before the police arrived. Just like they'd planned if the confession didn't work out and they were attacked.

The only part of the plan that had worked.

Cormac rushed to Teddy, helping her pull on an oversized shirt and some sweats, quickly zipping up his jeans and pulling her to him for a quick, silent hug before he jammed his feet into his scattered boots and went to help Wanda.

"I've got him, Wanda," Cormac whispered as he helped her up and away from an unconscious Stas, keeping his eyes on her face. "Dress. Hurry. He won't go anywhere."

Darnell ran from body to body, searching until he found Dennis, his face grim.

"What do we do next?" Cormac asked from the glass-covered floor where small fires burned, sending tendrils of acrid smoke upward to the ceiling.

Darnell dug into the deep pocket of his jeans and pulled out the recorder, instantly covered with blood from his fingers, and handed it to Cormac. "You give this to the po-po. Don't lose track of it. The rest, I got, man. Go. Be ready just like we planned," he urged with a slap to his shoulder before he turned and stooped to haul up Dennis's lifeless body. Throwing him over his shoulder, Darnell was gone in the blink of an eye.

Teddy knelt next to Marty, pushing her hair, soaked in blood and sweat, back from her face as she coaxed her arms into a sweater she'd never in a million years wear and begged her to put her pants and shoes on. "Please, Marty. I'll help you. Get dressed before the police get here. We have to stick to the plan."

Marty did as she was told, rushing and shaking as she did all the things she should, and then she was beside Nina again, stroking her hair, pressing her cheek to her friend's.

Teddy fought a scream of frustration and sorrow as she pressed the sleeve of her sweatshirt against Nina's wound, her breathing shallow and labored. "Where is the ambulance?" she asked, on the verge of hysteria. "We need help now!"

Suddenly the room filled with paramedics, who whisked Nina away on a sterile cot, hooking her up to an IV and blood-pressure cuff. The police entered right behind them, their eyes wide at the carnage, astonished that Cormac had Stas naked and pinned to the floor.

And there were questions, and more questions, and chaos, and crime-scene tape and chalk outlines and Cormac handing over the evidence they'd gathered, relaying the events of the night. There was Carmine, huddled and shaking so violently, he had to be carried out on a stretcher in handcuffs. And all Teddy could think was, she needed to get to the hospital to be with Nina.

And then she remembered Carl. Oh God. Where was Carl?

Carl, who'd done everything he was told to do, while looking almost catatonic. Teddy pushed her way through the throng of police and outside, where onlookers gawked. Cormac followed, gripping her hand to keep her close.

Then she saw him.

Propped weakly against a pole, his eyes wide, his torment crystal clear.

"Move!" she shouted to the people milling about him.

She reached out her hand to him, thrust it through the crowd and gripped his cold, stiff fingers, and he collapsed against her, his shoulders silently shaking.

Cormac sheltered them from behind, keeping the press and stray ambulance chasers from invading their circle.

Keeping them safe as Carl buried his face in her neck and they both cried.

Chapter 16

After they finished up the endless slew of questions the police lobbed at them, both alone and together, Teddy wanted to collapse, but as they entered the hospital, she knew she'd never sleep until she witnessed Nina was okay. There'd been plenty of questions, too. Like how four women and a man had overpowered Stas and his crew of gun-packers.

Somehow, they'd both managed to satisfy the police who seemed more interested in Carmine Ragusi and his wild tale of werewolves and bears.

Cormac pulled her close when she'd answered the last inquiry and the police wrapped things up and let her go—for now, according to them. There would be later questions she'd have to answer—questions they'd all have to answer.

"I can't believe he killed his partner like it was no big deal," Teddy mumbled. It had, in fact, been Mauricio who was murdered that night in the dealership, and Carmine had, in fact, led the police to believe it was his partner who was dabbling in the mob. Which led the police to keep things as quiet as possible.

During the course of the night, Carmine Ragusi confessed to the murder of his partner and the cover-up and his connections to Stas Vasilyev. He'd also revealed where his partner's body was buried, and that meant Mauricio's family would finally have some closure.

Teddy had heard a lot of mumbled chatter from his fellow police officers about Carmine and the story he told of bears and werewolves, all of which his now former colleagues were sure to talk about for years to come.

Cormac pressed a kiss to the top of her head. "That son of a bitch had some racket going on. It was a lot of cash."

To say the least. But Teddy didn't give a rat's ass about Carmine or Stas or anything else but Nina.

The nurses directed them to the waiting room on the third floor of the ICU and as they rode the elevator, Teddy sucked in gulps of air for courage. Covered in blood and smeared with black soot, she refused to give in to tears.

Nina needed all the strength she could gather, and she'd hate everyone crying over her.

Straightening her shoulders, Teddy saw the desk at the ICU was empty, so she and Cormac made a break for Nina's room unnoticed.

As they slipped inside, Teddy clung to Cormac's hand as he led her to an empty chair.

Marty sat next to her friend, and who Teddy assumed was Nina's husband, Greg, sat across from her. He was beautifully handsome, classically perfect in so many ways, just like Nina said. But his eyes...his eyes were haunted, riddled with agony, raw with emotion as he held his wife's hand next to his cheek.

Marty laid her head on Nina's belly, closing her eyes and gripping her friend's hand. "*Damn you, Statleon.* You should have just let me turn you when I offered. But no. Nooo. You were far too busy with buckets of chicken wings and brewskies to worry about the fact that you're not like us anymore. Too busy pretending to be a badass to realize there won't be any self-healing this time. You won't look at that fucking hole in your chest like all you need is a Band-Aid and a pint of O neg..."

Marty paused, her breath shuddering in and out of her lungs, her head lifting to reveal blue eyes filled with sorrow so deep, Teddy had to look away before she shattered in a million pieces.

Marty hadn't left Nina's side since they'd performed what Wanda had said was a tedious surgery. She had a broken arm from the fall, a break so ugly, she'd need pins and physical therapy to regain solid use of it. But worse was what that damn bullet had done. Stas's bullet had screamed through Nina's chest, just missing her heart, but the doctor warned their ragged crew, covered in blood and dirt, wet from the snow, that it could be touch and go.

If Nina made it through tonight, she had a fighting chance.

And then Marty shook her head as though she'd made a decision of some kind. "You'll need physical therapy and bed rest and it'll be a long road to recovery. So you can't do this anymore, Mistress of The Dark. As much as it hurts me to say that, you can't keep up with us and OOPS. Look at what happens when you try to keep up! You get your deaf ass shot. Didn't you hear me howl? Don't you know I can take a bullet in the chest but you can't? How could you be so damn stupid?" she hissed at her friend.

But then her voice softened, her words gentled. "You're not quick enough, strong enough, yet you're still the same stubborn pain in the ass you always were. But when you get your cheeseburger-eating, ice-cream-hording ass out of this bed, it stops. No more, because I can't...*I can't take it, Nina. I won't* take it! I'll never survive losing you..."

The heart monitor rang out a steady song, and Teddy was grateful for that. Nina was tough, maybe not vampire strong, but she was healthy and there was no way she'd believe anything other than this woman, this woman with her angry words and fierce loyalty, would be anything other than okay.

Marty pulled Nina's hand to her cheek, tears streaming from her eyes, rolling onto Nina's pale skin and dropping to the sheet covering her. "I begged you. I told you I didn't give a damn if it got me shunned or put me in werewolf jail or whatever the hell happens when you turn someone willfully. But you wouldn't listen, would you? Do you ever listen to me? No one had to know. You, with all your in-your-face, no-rules-apply-to-me bullshit, *refused*. The rule breaker was suddenly a chicken-shit. And now...look. Look at what you've done!" she whispered, her voice laced in hysteria, her shoulders shaking.

Wanda came up behind her friend and gripped her shoulders, her knuckles white from the effort, her face wet with tears mirroring Marty's.

And Teddy marveled at these women as tears also streamed down her face as well. Marveled at how true they were to each other. How steadfast. They were more than just family. They were something bigger. Something she had no definition for, no word in the dictionary covered how bonded these women were. How integral each of their lives was to the survival of the others.

It was amazing and frightening all at once.

"When you're done being a sissy-ass, lying around in this bed like some kind of diva, *you're done*. No more adventures for you, Elvira. If I have to lock you in a padded room, I'll damn well do it! You're not the person you were since the change, Nina. You have to stop pretending you are. Do you hear me in there?"

Teddy gnawed on the inside of her cheek to keep from crying out.

"I was so angry with you, Nina Statleon. I kept thinking, how could you *not* want us to turn you back? Why were chicken wings more important than living out our eternities together? What about Charlie and Greg? Didn't they matter? How could you go right on being human when you'd eventually die and leave us?" She rasped the words, pressing Nina's hand to her forehead.

Wanda grabbed Marty's free hand and clung to it, held on to it like her life depended on the very contact.

"Then I thought you were choosing. I thought all the horrible things you always say to us just might have a smidge of truth. Maybe you really were glad you were human again because it meant you didn't have to put up with us for an eternity. *With me.* Or maybe you weren't really as passionate about helping others like us as we were. But that wasn't it at all. I know the truth now, Nina. Darnell told me tonight. You were too afraid I'd get caught for turning you—that I'd end up punished, maybe taken away from Keegan and Hollis because it was my second infraction, after helping turn Wanda. I didn't understand it at the time. But you were just looking out for me. Just like always. *Please* come back, and I swear on every damn eyeshadow I own, I'll look out for *you* now. Always. No matter what. For as long as you choose to be here."

Teddy stuffed her fist against her mouth to keep from weeping out loud, the hot sting of tears clouding her eyes. Cormac pulled her from her chair and sat, bringing her to his lap, settling her against him. His big hand ran over her hair, pass after pass, soothing her.

And the night wore on. Long, dark, cold, sterile, with nothing but the glow of monitors and the incessant beep of Nina's life in green numbers on a black screen.

She prayed. She made bargains with whoever was in charge. She offered up sacrifices. Whatever it took to keep Nina with them, she'd give it up.

Marty and Wanda never moved. Clinging to one another, they talked in whispers to their friend, stroked her hair, held vigil. Greg sat in silence, his eyes closed, his wife's hand at his forehead.

Teddy and Cormac brought a tormented Carl to the waiting room, where they took turns talking to him, reassuring him. Exhausted, he finally spread his long body over a row of chairs and placed his head on Teddy's lap, where she caressed the face that had so rapidly become precious to her until he slept.

Darnell and Archibald had joined them, holding hands, the wide beefy paw of the demon swallowing up the smaller manservant's fingers. Darnell's lips moved, likely in silent prayer. Something she no longer found quite so strange.

Archibald, as perfectly dressed as ever, sat straight as an arrow, his posture impeccable, everything in its place but his tears. They streamed freely from his eyes, plopping to the black linen of his trousers in salty splotches.

Her brothers had finally arrived, travel-weary, their eyes brimming with worry when they enveloped her in a silent hug then shook Cormac's hand before they, too, sat to wait.

Nurses came and went. Doctors on silent feet tended to patients. The day came and went, too, melding into yet another night of waiting.

No one but Carl slept. No one spoke much. Every ounce of energy, words, thoughts, were reserved for Nina alone.

The sudden rush of footsteps and carts from across the hall aimed at Nina's room had everyone sitting up straight and holding their breath.

Cormac squeezed her hand and she squeezed his back as sheer terror made her tense up.

So she closed her eyes and kicked her prayers up a notch.

Please, whoever does whatever when running this big ol' place we call the universe, get the person in charge. Tell them not to let Nina die. I'm begging you. I'll do whatever you want, give you whatever you want, but she's here because she was helping us. If it wasn't for us, she'd be at home right now eating chicken wings and slugging one back in her kitchen.

She has a baby. A small, beautiful baby who needs her mother. She has friends who need her. A husband. She counts. Her selflessness counts. Please, after everything she's done for everyone else, please, don't let her die.

Amen.

The silence from Nina's room left Teddy the closest she'd come to breaking since this had begun. She clung even tighter to Cormac's hand, squeezing her eyes shut and willing someone in that room to come out and tell them everything was going to be all right.

And then the door swung open.

"I said get the hell off me, Dr. Frankenstein! Jesus. That damn thing is cold. And would it kill you lot to bring me some food? Marty, stop touching my hair! And quit your blubberin'. It makes you look like a blowfish, all puffy and red—"

Everyone jumped up at once, cheering so loud, the nurse from the station down the hall came running and warned them to simmer down.

There was hugging, noisy tears, noses blowing, but most importantly, there was gratitude.

And Nina. Alive. Well. Mouthy as always.

Cormac gathered her in his arms and hugged her tight. "The ex-vampire, she lives to snark another day."

She let her head fall to his shoulder and smiled. "Isn't it amazing?"

Wrapping his arms around her waist, he rested his chin on top of her head. "Just as amazing as you."

"I'm pretty average. Also, I've never come back from the almost dead. Or even the undead. Nina wins."

"A very fair point. You know, you were pretty badass in that bar last tonight, Teddy Bear. I gotta give it to you for taking on two of them at once."

"Dennis is dead," she croaked, still unable to believe it.

Cormac stiffened against her. "I had no choice. He would have killed you. No way was I going to let that happen."

She shivered when she remembered what Dennis would have done if not for Cormac's interference. "Thank you. I don't know if I'll ever be able to thank you enough for saving my life."

"Well, you helped save mine. Fair is fair, and remind me to never make you angry. The way you were reaming Carmine a new one, waving that gun around? Impressive stuff, honey."

"I was so angry at feeling so helpless, I got overwhelmed. It just knocked me for a loop."

"It's over now. All of it is finally over."

For the first time in what felt like forever, she took a deep breath.

Cormac nudged her. "So what are ya gonna do, now that you're free from a murder rap, Theodora Gribanov?"

"Go to Disneyland. Duh."

"How about maybe we just do coffee over some breakfast? I don't think I'm up for the Harry Potter ride after last night."

"Are you asking me out, Cormac Vitali?"

"The first of many times."

She chuckled against his dirty flannel shirt. "You're kinda cute, ya know? Wanna be my life mate?"

"Only if it means I get the right side of the bed. Oh, and that I can leave the toilet seat up."

She leaned back in his embrace and tweaked his beard with a grin. "Better hit Craigslist for a new life mate, buddy. Toilet seats are deal breakers."

"They have life mates on Craigslist? Shut the front freakin' door. All this time I thought I had no choice in the matter. I thought it was you or nothing," he teased, cupping the back of her head to tilt her face upward.

Pressing her palm to Cormac's jaw, she winked when she ran her thumb over his beard. "Oh, you have a choice, mister."

"Is it 'bend to my will or die while I dance in your intestines'?"

Her laughter rang out in the small waiting room. "Well, that's a choice, isn't it?"

Brushing his lips against hers, he whispered, "Then I choose you, Theodora Gribanov. I choose *you*."

And that was all Teddy, the soon-to-be ex-bounty hunter, needed to hear.

* * *

Three months later

Teddy, Toni, and Cormac sat in the hushed courtroom where Cormac and Toni were preparing to testify at a grand jury hearing to prosecute Stas Vasilyev and Carmine Ragusi for the murder of Mauricio Benneducci.

After handing over their recorded evidence to the police, and enduring months of questioning, flying back and forth from Colorado to New Jersey to meet with law enforcement official after law enforcement official, an amazing, mind-blowing trip to Shamalot to collect Toni, and a full-on investigation of every detail of their lives, Cormac, Toni, and Teddy had struck a deal with prosecutors for immunity.

Now all that was needed to close this chapter of their lives was their testimony to put Carmine, Stas, and his crew of foul thugs away forever. That day was today.

That night in the bar, when everything had finally come to a screeching halt, still came back in fits and spurts in Teddy's dreams. The screaming, the gunfire, Dennis dead at her feet, the horrifying moment, suspended forever in her mind's eye, when Nina was shot...all of it stuck to her like static cling.

But Cormac was also there, soothing her fears, talking it out with her as they helped each other to mend. And they were growing, learning, laughing.

His reunion with Toni was only one word in Teddy's mind. Magical. Toni had cried when she'd flung herself at Cormac, cleansing tears of relief. He'd hugged her tight and then introduced Teddy as his girlfriend, and Toni had introduced her fiancé Iver.

And they'd laughed, cried, talked about their parents, reminisced about when they were kids—healed.

If in her wildest dreams, she ever thought it possible to step into a fairytale, stepping into Shamalot had fulfilled every expectation. It was all the things little girls imagine and more, and meeting Toni for the first time had been about as perfect as perfect could get.

She was still adjusting to a giant blue ogre, and Toni's fiancé, Prince Iver, who made her giggle endlessly with his curiosity about all things Jersey and modern-day contraptions and his pattern of speech, wherein he called her Lady Theodora.

As the courtroom stirred and the judge took the stand, Teddy gripped Cormac's hand, looking down at the missing digit—a stark reminder of why they were here to begin with. The last thing she wanted to do was get up in front of a bunch of people and be hammered one more time about the events of that night. But she'd do it because it helped Cormac and Toni.

Testifying today brought up all her old insecurities, all the old questions about her character and how strong she really was, if she could have stayed with Dennis as long as she had.

Stas scared the hell out of her in the same way Dennis did, and now the chance to tell the world was at her feet. But she felt intimidated and small. Exactly the way Dennis had made her feel.

No. She remembered Nina's words after a long Skype call. That was the way she'd *allowed* him to make her feel, and she wasn't ever going to allow anyone a repeat performance. Who was smaller than Dennis, Nina'd asked her? A man who'd verbally assaulted her time and again and then beat the living hell out of her because he couldn't have what he wanted? Nina repeatedly reminded her she was a strong, confident woman, and no one could take that unless she let them.

When Cormac was called to the stand, Toni leaned over and winked at her, gripping her cold fingers, her smile warm and so confident when she whispered, "You got this, Teddy. This is the beginning of your future—free and clear. Now, chin up, chest out, head held high. *Always* be the hunter, honey."

Always be the hunter.

Teddy gripped Toni's hand and squeezed when Cormac took his place on the stand before the microphone.

Nina's words from outside the courtroom just moments ago replayed in her head. *We'll be right outside, Teddy Bear. All of us. You need us, you say the word. But you won't need us, kiddo. Because you're a mighty bitch who's a badass with a dart gun who helped take down a goddamn mobster. Nobody fucks with bitches like that.*

Yeah. Nobody fucks with bitches like that.

She heard the bailiff swear Cormac in and held her breath.

"Do you, Cormac Vitali, solemnly swear to tell the truth, the whole truth, and nothing but the truth, so help you God?"

"I do," he said, looking directly at Teddy, his voice strong and clear.

And that was when Teddy felt the surge of power, the one she'd struggled so long to recapture, sizzling through her veins, spreading through her limbs, re-centering itself right back where it belonged.

At her core.

With her chin up, chest out, and her head held high, Teddy prepared to walk into the beginning of her future with Cormac and her new friends.

Because she always wanted to be the hunter. Strong and sure—with Cormac hunting right beside her—forever.

Epilogue

Four months, twelve and counting utterly implausible, zany paranormal accidents gone by—a chicken-wing-loving, beer-guzzling, recuperating-from-a-wound-that-almost-ended-her-life-but-saved-her-friends ex-vampire; a beautiful halfsie with the gift of mediation and an endless supply of eye rolls; a gorgeous blonde werewolf who will never let her bestie live down the fact that she took a bullet for her; a cuddly demon who was teaching the sweetest zombie on the face of the planet how to slow dance; a manservant, busily making sure every last detail of his scrumptious buffet was perfect; a gorgeous, fiery-haired almost princess and her handsome Prince Iver; various accidentally turned guests, such as dragons and genies and cougars, oh my; a string of fairytale creatures, like big blue ogres and little old ladies named Roz; one unaware-she's-about-to-be-ambushed brown bear; and a handsome grizzly in a cheesy blue tuxedo with matching ruffles, gathered for a very special surprise first date at the newly renovated place the new couple called their home away from home...

"Surprise!" voices yelled from the dark interior of the penguin pool house at Sanctuary, just as muted globe lights popped on and a soft love song began to drift to Teddy's ears.

"Happy prom!" Marty and Wanda squealed, gathering her into a rhinestoned hug of blue and gold tulle-covered satin and clouds of musky-sweet perfume.

Nina held up a dress. A very familiar dress. And she wore a dress, too. Granted, she wore her black hoodie over the top of it and work boots, but a beautiful red dress was beneath the sweatshirt, swaying at her ankles and hugging her long legs.

"What is all this?" Teddy asked, breathless.

Nina shook the dress under her nose with the arm not in a sling, and grinned, her white teeth flashing. "Happy prom, kiddo!"

Teddy smiled at her friend and occasional animal consultant, giving her the hug she knew would annoy her. "Hey, lady! How are you feeling?"

Nina's recuperation from the bullet she'd taken was indeed slower than even the ex-vampire expected. Nothing moved as quickly as it once did for Nina, not her healing or her body, and it frustrated her. According to her doctors, physical therapy for her arm was going quite well, despite the names she called her hunky Swedish therapist, who laughed off her ire-filled rants.

But what Teddy worried most about was Nina's mind, her emotional state. "So have you given thought to what we talked about?"

Nina made a face. "You mean more therapy? Like maybe a fucking couch and a bottle of Xanax?"

"No. I mean talking about your feelings with a skilled professional, Heathen. A *paranormal* professional."

They'd cornered Nina shortly after her accident and broached the subject of seeking counseling for how displaced she was feeling. Someone to talk to who could help her cope with her fears about leaving this world before her baby and her husband, her friends.

She'd spouted all the typical Nina protests until Teddy mentioned how she'd someday have to explain to Charlie and Carl, who didn't totally understand mortality as it pertained to Nina, why she wasn't immortal and they were, and that was the tipping point to her reconsidering. Nothing was more important to Nina than Charlie and Carl.

"Feelings-schmeelings. I hate fucking talking about how I feel. I feel fine."

"*Nina...*" Teddy warned as Marty and Wanda rolled their eyes. "If I can be strong, so can you. Always be the hunter."

Nina scrunched up her beautiful face. "Oh, shut the fuck up. I said I'd go and I'll GD go. But for now, c'mon, we gotta get ya all dolled up and slap some crap on your face so you can cry it all off when you're slow dancing to some sappy shit. Bust a move, Teddy Bear. Your man's gonna be here any minute."

Teddy fought tears as she took the dress Nina held out to her. Everything made sense to her now. "So, that's what that shopping trip last week was about?"

Just last week, the three of them had flown in with Carl and stayed the weekend at the ranch with Teddy and her brothers. She'd given them the tour of the newly renovated Sanctuary, shown them the sights, watched as Nina bonded with the horses at the ranch and at Sanctuary, and they'd taken her shopping for a total makeover.

There'd been creams and lotions, lip gloss after lip gloss, a hair appointment with some fancy man with a fancy French accent and magical scissors.

There was squealing over her hair, finally trimmed and layered in a style that made her feel like a princess, and sales and discount designer malls and a final stop at an exclusive boutique, where the women had tried on dresses for an upcoming graduation for Wanda's niece, Naomi.

Wanda told her they were going to surprise Naomi with a prom dress, and being that Teddy was Naomi's size, asked if she'd try dresses on in her stead. They'd coaxed her into giving them her opinion because they claimed they were old and outdated and if anyone in the group was even remotely close to Naomi's age, it was Teddy.

She'd happily obliged, trying on at least twenty dresses before she made an entrance in the last one of the day—the one that made all the women sigh with pleasure, even Nina.

It was strapless and mint green, with a bodice covered in iridescent pink rhinestones. The skirt was bell-shaped, cinched at her waist and made out of a combination of mint-green tulle and silk that floated around her knees like a whispered caress.

Everyone had agreed Naomi would love it, and Wanda had shelled out far more money than Teddy had dedicated to ten years' worth of clothing, and they'd left to join her brothers and Cormac for dinner.

Marty cupped her jaw and smiled. She looked like a fairy princess with her hair falling around her face in soft waves, gleaming against her sapphire-blue dress. She held up a curling iron and Wanda dangled a makeup bag. "Let's get this show on the road. It's princess time!"

Teddy barely had time to process her surroundings before they had her in her office, where curling irons heated and makeup was pulled from a bag and set on her desk. Eyeshadow brushes worked their magic, slick gloss slid over her lips, shoes appeared out of nowhere, sparkly and probably two inches too dangerously high for someone as clumsy as her.

Marty curled and fluffed her hair, and Wanda spritzed and chatted happily while Nina steamed her gown. And then they were tugging off her old denim shirt and ordering her out of her jeans and dropping the dress—the most beautiful dress she'd ever seen—over her head.

Pulling her into her office's private bathroom, they pushed her toward the wide mirror, where her breathing hitched.

"Ohhhh," she murmured. Unable to believe this was her reflection. Her hair, now a mixture of platinum and caramel highlights, sat high atop her head in soft curls that fell in all the right places around her face.

Her eyes, once a plain hazel, now looked mysterious and smoldering beneath the deep brown and green smoky eye Wanda had created with eyeshadow and mascara. Her lips shone peachy-pink, glossed and pouty; her cheekbones highlighted by a sparkling peachy glaze of something Marty said was a new product at Pack.

But the dress. Her dress stole the show. It was perfect, hugging her curves in all the right places, while lifting her breasts and shimmering in a dreamy confection of fabric.

"You look amazing, sweetie," Marty said from behind her, gripping her shoulders and squeezing.

Wanda gave her a warm hug, too. "Our little Teddy is all grown up, girls. Isn't she beautiful?" she asked with a hitch in her voice.

"You fucking look like Cinderella, Teddy Bear. Ask me, I'm pretty sure I met her doppelganger in Shamalot," Nina said, pinching her cheek with affection before pulling a bag of Goobers from her hoodie pocket and dropping some in her mouth.

Teddy turned from the mirror, her eyes brimming with tears. "You did all of this for me?"

Marty whipped a tissue from the inside of her bodice and dabbed at Teddy's eyes. "Don't cry now, you'll muss your makeup. And yes, we had a little something to do with it."

She squeezed Marty's hand. "*Something?*"

Wanda smiled coquettishly and held out a long gold box with a tiny gold bow. "Yes, something. Now, this is from the three of us. Wear it with all our love. We have to hurry, so open it!"

Teddy popped open the box to reveal a note inside. She cocked her head when she unfolded the paper.

Her mouth fell open. She blinked her eyes twice and reread the slip of paper. "It's the deed. The deed to…Sanctuary?"

Nina used the heel of her good hand to knock Teddy in the shoulder. "You didn't think we were gonna let all those damn eagles and monkeys and giraffes and shit be shipped off to some jackasses who don't know what the fuck they're doin', did ya?"

Her heart throbbed in her chest as she gaped at them. "Wait. You bought Sanctuary for me?" she squeaked out in disbelief. "But you donated all that money to the renovations already! If it wasn't for you, Mr. Noodles wouldn't have an enclosure, let alone a sign language teacher. You already paid a fortune to help here. I can't let you buy—"

"The fuck you can't, Sunshine. Look, kiddo. We're rich. All of us. Like no-joke, make-it-rain-cash rich. You're our friend. You needed help. We helped. This ain't nuthin' but a blip in our bank accounts and it's for a good cause I can get behind. Plus, you and Cormac are a damned good investment as far as we're concerned. Now take the fucking deed. You and Pooh Bear go off and save all the furry and/or winged babies you can with the peace of mind that this shit is yours. And never forget, Mr. Noodles the monkey is my boyfriend. He needed someone to help him express himself so he'd quit flingin' poop at little Jo-Jo out of anger. He was frustrated is all. I get that. My primate man gets only the best if I have shit to say about it."

When the women had first come to the shambles of Sanctuary, just shortly after they'd taken down Stas, and Cormac and Toni were preparing to testify against him, Teddy had been in the process of trying to find last-minute investors who'd donate money to save the place she loved.

Checkbooks had flown from purses as each woman had donated a hefty sum. Sums big enough to allow Teddy to pay off the bank and take care of some of the more pressing structural issues haunting Sanctuary. Then they'd called their friends and they'd donated, too.

Mr. Noodles, the Macaque monkey, had taken one look at Nina cooing up at him from the ground and lobbed a pile of his lunch—a lunch that had just exited his back end—right at her head. But Nina didn't get angry. Instead, she'd climbed the tree he sat in with one hand, against their protests about her recent injuries, and talked to him for two solid hours and even though Mr. Noodles was deaf and couldn't hear a word she said, he'd curled into her arm and wouldn't let go.

She agreed, because he was deaf and his mother had abandoned him, leaving him incapable of surviving on his own, that he was just misunderstood, and she'd set about finding someone skilled enough to teach a monkey sign language—which, it turned out, Mr. Noodles learned quickly. His anger turned to productivity right before Teddy and Cormac's eyes.

Nina, Charlie, Carl and Greg skyped with Mr. Noodles every week now without fail to check on his progress.

"Thank you," she whispered. "I'll never be able to thank you enough for this. For everything. For saving both Cormac and me. For giving me back the place I love almost more than anywhere else."

Carl poked his head inside the bathroom, two of Sanctuary's parrots, Kanye and Kim, sitting contentedly on his shoulder. The zombie loved animals as much as Nina and his uncanny ability to soothe them, communicate with them, had Teddy dialing him up on more than one occasion since they'd been back to ask for his advice when she struggled with a new rescue.

She couldn't help but notice how smart and mature he looked in his tuxedo, with his hair brushed over his forehead and his shiny cufflinks winking under the bathroom light.

Carl thumped her on her shoulder and held out his arms, pulling her into a crooked hug full of his particular brand of warmth. Then he pointed to the watch on his wrist. "Ur…" He struggled with the word.

Teddy cupped his jaw to reassure him. "Go slow. I can wait."

Carl had managed to express to Nina how frustrating it was for him to keep people waiting when he attempted verbal conversations—because Carl was always worried about everyone else's comfort but his own.

Nina and Greg had considered a signing teacher, but Carl had trouble keeping his fingers glued to his hand; bending them to sign was likely going to prove difficult.

So instead, Teddy reminded him that she didn't mind waiting at all, due to the fact that when Carl spoke, he didn't need a lot of words to fill up a conversation. What he managed to say was always valued and important without the hindrance of frills.

Carl smiled and repeated, stuttered and broken, "Uur—eeee."

"Hurryuphurryuphurryup!" Kanye squawked impatiently, dancing along Carl's shoulder.

Teddy laughed, straightening his boutonniere. "What am I hurrying about?"

Carl took her by the hand, tucking it under his arm. "This way." He tugged her back out of the office and down the long hall.

As she entered the penguin room, where waterfalls trickled out their tune and Suits the penguin waddled up and down the paths leading to the beautiful new pool just recently installed, she saw Cormac.

Dressed in a blue tux with blue ruffles, holding a corsage in his hand, so handsome her teeth ached from just looking at him.

He held out his arms to her and she rushed into them, burying her face in his broad chest, just the way she'd done so many times before.

"For you," he said, holding up the wrist corsage made of mint-green and white carnations.

She held out her hand with a smile and let him slide it over her wrist. "It's beautiful. Thank you."

He'd been right about their getting to know each other. They'd spent hours and hours full of movies and lunch dates, dinners made up of Porterhouse steaks, walks in the forest, and visits to the cabin where their relationship had begun.

They laughed, they talked, they even had a couple of fights. They made out like teenagers, they slow-danced under the Colorado stars. They moved Cormac into an apartment and continued to fight a long, hard battle with his credit card companies to get his ruined credit back in order, with Lenny Kravitz always on his computer desk, purring.

They spent days working on the rebirth of Sanctuary, making phone calls, overseeing the construction of new habitats, plowing toward a mutual goal just like Cormac had promised.

They created a routine all their own. One they could count on, day in and day out, no matter what, and they never missed dinner together, whether it was at the ranch with her brothers or at Cormac's place.

And now they were here—together—at her prom.

"Did you do all this for *me*?" Teddy managed to squeak out as she lifted her head and took in the clusters of balloons in pastel colors floating about the room. Lights twinkled from corner to corner, a DJ played 98 Degrees, streamers in rainbow colors swayed from the ceiling, and a banner reading *Teddy's Big Excellent Prom* hung from the long string of tall windows overlooking the grounds.

"For our first official date," Cormac said on a warm smile, pulling her to the dance floor in the center of everything and twirling her around. "But I didn't do it alone. I did it with the girls and Carl and Arch. All refreshments courtesy of Archibald and Carl, in fact."

She giggled. "But we've had a million dates since we got back to Colorado."

Pressing a gentle kiss to her lips, Cormac shook his head. "Ah, but we didn't have this one. This one is special."

"So you planned this? All of this?" she asked, as he pulled her tight to him and grinned down at her.

"Yep. Right down to the rainforest theme."

Teddy sighed and kissed him hard. "Thank you. It's beautiful."

"Speaking of beautiful, have I told you how beautiful you look tonight?"

Her hand went to the floaty dress, swishing at her knees. "Courtesy of Marty, Nina, and Wanda."

"It's amazing. *You're* amazing," he whispered.

Melting against him, Teddy wondered what had inspired this. "What made you choose a prom?"

"You remember that night Arch gave us that whacky tea?"

She chuckled and nodded, snuggling closer and inhaling his cologne. "I do. You saw a unicorn. Did we ever name the unicorn?"

"I'm still thinking on it, but do you remember telling me you never went to your prom?"

Her heart melted. He'd listened to her when she'd said she was too embarrassed to ask her brothers to buy her a dress because money had been so tight. He'd *listened*.

Teddy wrinkled her nose. "Ugh. I'm convinced it was the tea that made me do it. Kinda pathetic, huh?"

Cormac caressed her cheek with his big palm. "Not even a little. I remember thinking I wanted to give you back something every girl should experience at least once. But I also wanted you to always remember this night for more than one reason. I have ulterior motives."

Closing her eyes, she wrapped her arms around his neck and counted her blessings. "Ooo, an ulterior motive? Do tell."

Bracketing her face, he slowed their movement and looked into her eyes. "I wanted you to always remember the night I told you I've fallen crazy in love with you, Theodora Gribanov. I wanna do this life mate thing so hard we hurt it."

Her heart throbbed in her chest, but she looked him right in the eye and whispered on a happy sigh, "I love you, too, Cormac. Let's put the hurt on this life mate thing."

Cormac's lips pressed against hers, his tongue slipping into her mouth, sending a thrill of yearning to her heart. "So you know what this means, right?"

"Does this mean I have to lose my virginity to you after we get drunk on spiked punch?"

"Don't you have to still have that to lose it?" he teased against her mouth.

"So fresh, Vitali. Knock it off or I won't let you get to second base."

"Which brings me to this—I don't know about you, but I was wondering if it might be time to, you know, consider sealing the deal?" He winked comically at her.

"Seal a deal? Whatever do you mean, Mr. Vitali?" she joked, knowing exactly what he meant.

They'd chosen to wait to make love. There had been many grueling nights when they'd almost caved due to their raging hormones, but they wanted the time to be right. For the physical expression of their relationship to mean something.

For love and total commitment to be their motivation.

Curving his arm around her waist, Cormac hauled her closer, letting her feel what he meant. "You know exactly what I mean. Don't torture me. Either you're in or you're out."

"Isn't this the part of my teen dream where I crash to reality when I remember guys say whatever they have to in order to get in your pants?" she asked, running her fingers over his arms and luxuriating in his muscles.

He ran his lips over her neck, making her shiver with anticipation. "You don't have pants on. And I'm crushed. Do you really think I would say 'I love you' to just get you into bed? Have you no soul?"

Her head fell back on her shoulders as she laughed. "That's what I wanted to hear. Tonight could just be your lucky night."

He growled playfully at her, swirling her around the dance floor as everyone joined them. Music played, the girls and their husbands danced, and Vadim and Viktor did the limbo. Carl asked one of her staff members to dance; Darnell did the outdated but hysterical robot. Toni and her fiancé Prince Iver ruled the chicken dance, and Arch did an amazing twist, outlasting every one of them on the floor.

It was a night full of magic, full of promise, full of all the people and animals she loved most.

Several hours and some weenies in a blanket later, back at Cormac's apartment, he pulled her into his bedroom, where he'd lit dozens of candles and had a bottle of wine chilling in a bucket.

The room, swathed in a soft, flickering glow, was enchanting, leaving her breathless at the care he'd taken to make tonight perfect. He'd made up his big bed with soft pillows and a thick comforter and placed a pink, fuzzy bathrobe on the chair in the corner.

"As if you hadn't already outdone yourself," she whispered, tears forming at the corners of her eyes.

Cormac popped the cork on the wine and poured her a glass, handing it to her with a hot kiss that made her toes curl.

Teddy reached up and loosened his bowtie as she took a sip, before she set it down and grabbed the lapels of his jacket, pushing it from his wide shoulders. Her hands ached to touch his flesh, experience him in his entirety, the way she'd fantasized each time he took his shirt off when he was working on a project at Sanctuary or when he wore a pair of jeans that made his already outstanding butt look even more outstanding.

With fingers she couldn't believe were capable of unbuttoning his ruffled shirt, as shaky as they were, Teddy swiftly worked her way down the length of it until her hands were smoothing over his chest, palming his hot flesh.

He groaned, gripping her wrists and slinging them around his neck as he pulled her close and unzipped her dress.

She stepped out of it, left with nothing but her heels and a pair of pale pink panties; she tried not to shy away from his deep gaze.

Cormac groaned his appreciation, his eyes darkening, devouring her as he unbuckled his belt and kicked off his blue trousers, leaving him in only his black boxer-briefs.

He was as beautiful as she'd imagined; all thick ripples of muscle, tight abs, and that delicious carved-out hipbone she wanted to run her tongue over.

His legs were thick and lightly sprinkled with crisp dark hair, bulging thighs that tapered to well-muscled calves. He took a step toward her just as she did the same and their skin touched for the first time.

Dakota Cassidy | Bearly Accidental

Teddy hissed her pleasure, clutching at Cormac's shoulders just as he moaned against her mouth, kissing her deeply, driving his tongue against her, rasping the silky instrument along the outline of her mouth.

Hands explored flesh, skimming, discovering, relishing the freedom their fingers were finally allowed.

Cormac's index fingers slipped inside the leg of her panties on both sides, whispering over her skin, teasing her until her back arched and he pulled her to the bed.

Setting her on the soft comforter, he gazed down at her, pulling his boxer-briefs off then removing her panties.

He hissed appreciatively again when she was in nothing but her heels, falling to his knees on the bed to part her thighs and settle between them. Teddy's hands went to his thick hair, clutching strands of it and bucking when his breath grazed her most sensitive flesh, sighing as his beard scratched over her legs.

His kiss was slow, gentle, his chest rumbling on an approving groan when his tongue flicked out to taste her, making Teddy clench her eyes shut in anticipation for what was to come. Cormac took his time, parting her flesh in slow increments, stroking, licking, pulling her closer to his mouth until he slid his hands beneath her ass and she was flush against his tongue.

Her legs rose of their own accord, wrapping around his shoulders, her back arching into his delicious thrusts. When he slipped his finger inside her, Teddy saw stars, flashes of color behind her eyelids before she whimpered her pleasure, bucking against him.

White-hot heat pooled in her belly, snaking upward, making her nipples tighten until she exploded. She rode the crest of her orgasm, fighting the urge to scream her delight, gripping the comforter on either side of her as she came.

The sweet torture was like a tidal wave of pleasure, lifting her up then dragging her under, leaving her boneless and weak.

Cormac kneaded her thighs, massaging the muscles to ease the tension until she felt like a puddle of melted butter, but her hands itched to touch him, to experience the most intimate parts of his body.

Tugging on his wide shoulders, she dragged him upward, his chest scraping her tight nipples, his abs pressing into the soft flesh of her belly. When his mouth took hers again, the urge to order him to make love to her was strong, but she resisted in favor of slowing down and making this first time together last.

Rolling him to his back, she pinned him with a thigh around his legs, pulling his head close for another kiss, running her hands over his sleek lines until she reached his cock. Long and hard, he pulsed against her fingertips when she let them skim the hot flesh.

Cormac cupped her breast, running his thumb over her nipple, tweaking it, sending shooting waves of heat to her core, renewing her lust, stoking the embers of her desire.

Her pulse raced as she tried to slow this aching need, this agonizing want to have him inside her. Bracing her hands on his chest, Teddy slithered down along his body, sighing at the skin-to-skin contact, until she was at his hip, pulling at him and encouraging him to roll toward her.

She wasted no time in enveloping his cock between her hands, her fingers grasping him firmly, twisting upward and back down along the length again. He writhed against her when she sipped at his silken flesh, kissing him, licking, before she took him into her mouth.

Cormac tensed, his body rigid from the moment the heat of her lips surrounded him, and then he moaned, long and low, muttering something unintelligible.

He dragged his hand through her hair, pulling her close when she cupped his testicles, gently kneading them, running her tongue over his cock until his hips rolled against her, pushing, driving, thrusting.

"*No more,*" he panted, husky and deep, pulling his hips back from her, gripping her shoulders.

Teddy wrapped her arms around his shoulders and hauled herself up along his body, pinning him to the bed, capturing his mouth as she straddled him.

As she looked down at him, this man she'd fallen so deeply in love with, her chest tightened when he caught her watching him. He let his fingers walk along her arm and up toward her mouth. Pressing them to her lips, he said, "I love you."

She caught his hand in hers, cupping it against her cheek, and closed her eyes, inhaling the scent that was all Cormac. "*I love you, too, Cormac.*"

His moan of urgency made her lift her hips, allowing him the space to move beneath her and settle at her entrance.

This was the moment she'd waited four months for. The moment when they'd become one. Holding her breath, Teddy leaned back, snapping a picture in her mind of their flesh, his darker, hers lighter, preparing to connect.

Cormac's first thrust upward made her gasp, stretched her, making her brace the heels of her hands on his chest as she adjusted.

That moment, that magically sweet moment when they connected, was sheer bliss. Her eyes rolled to the back of her head, her body swaying in his arms, which had come up around her to keep her from pitching backward.

Strong and sure, she gripped his forearms and raised her hips, thrusting downward on his cock, whimpering at how completely he filled her.

And then they found their rhythm, the special place where two people who connect meet and find completion.

Cormac felt it, too. She knew he did when his eyes opened wide and filled with surprise, before they became heavy with desire and he lifted his head to capture one of her nipples, rolling his tongue over the beaded bud.

Wrapping her arms around his head, Teddy cradled him close as their flesh met and pulled away, their chests rose and fell, their breathing became raspy.

That rush of heat assaulted her again, threading along her veins, pulsing in ripples of need until she knew she couldn't hold on much longer.

Cormac's last thrust, slick and white-hot, drove her to the brink, the pleasure so intense, she cried out and gripped his shoulders. "Cormac!"

The world titled, tipped, crashed around her. The pounding of her pulse in her ears drowned out everything else. Everything but Cormac and the steady beat of his heart and his moans of pleasure as he, too, found release.

As the last vestiges of her climax subsided, Teddy clung to him, tears stinging her eyes. One managed to escape and roll down her cheek, plopping against his face.

He brought his hands up to her face, bracketing it with his wide palms, wiping her cheek with his thumb with a smile before cradling her in his arms.

As Cormac pulled her tight, he gave her a light nudge. "Well, I think we consummated the life mate thing all right and proper, don't you?

She giggled against his chest and rolled her eyes. "Oh, indeed. Totally worth the grueling four-month wait."

Rolling her to her back, Cormac gazed down at her and grinned. "Whaddya say we make up for lost time?"

Tweaking his beard, Teddy grinned back. "Wow. Again? You're quite the stud, Vitali."

"You've been driving me crazy for months, Gribanov," he murmured against her lips, slipping his arms under her waist.

She pressed her fingers to his lips to keep him at bay for just a moment longer. "Wait. Seriously. Tonight was everything a prom could be and more. Have I said thank you for making me feel like I'm the most important person in the world?"

Kissing her fingertips, Cormac smiled. "You *are* the most important person in my world. Well, you and Nee-Nee the giraffe. I'm just telling you right now, if anyone can give you a run for your money, it's gonna be her. Have you seen the way she bats her eyelashes at me? Crushes me. She's damn well irresistible."

Nee-Nee, the one-eyed giraffe, adored Cormac. When she saw him from an acre away, she came running. "Am I gonna have to take a bitch down with my dart gun?" she teased, kissing the corner of his mouth.

He mock-shivered, his eyes gleaming. "Oooo, I like it when you get all *Raiders of The Lost Ark* on me. It's hot."

"There were no dart guns in *Raiders of The Lost Ark*. And just you remember who you belong to, buddy."

"Oh, trust me, I'm not ever going to forget the woman who threw me over her shoulder after knocking me out, then rather than ask if I had anything to say about it, *told* me I was her life mate. Not ever. I've been properly owned."

"Owned forever?" she asked, snuggling under him, more incredibly happy than she'd ever been.

"*Forever*, or at least until you retire that damn dart gun." He laughed at his own joke.

And then she couldn't help but laugh, too.

But the best part was when they laughed together—in the way only two people who were true life mates do.

The End
(For now!)

Author Note: Thank you so much for reading *Bearly Accidental*! I hope you'll all come back and join me for a quick jaunt into Nina's head (don't be too afraid) when she finally, after much pressure from her BFFs, seeks professional advice from a renowned paranormal therapist who's willing to help Nina get through this new transition in her life, in *How Nina Got Her Fang Back*, coming in the summer of 2016!

Note from Dakota

I do hope you enjoyed this book, I'd so appreciate it if you'd help others enjoy it too.

Recommend it. Please help other readers find this book by recommending it.

Review it. Please tell other readers why you liked this book by reviewing it at online retailers or your blog. Reader reviews help my books continue to be valued by distributors/resellers. I adore each and every reader who takes the time to write one!

If you love the book or leave a review, please email dakota@dakotacassidy.com so I can thank you with a personal email. Your support means more than you'll ever know! Thank you!

About Dakota

Dakota Cassidy is a *USA Today* bestselling author with over thirty books. She writes laugh-out-loud cozy mysteries, romantic comedy, grab-some-ice erotic romance, hot and sexy alpha males, paranormal shifters, contemporary kick-ass women, and more.

Dakota was invited by Bravo TV to be the Bravoholic for a week, wherein she snarked the hell out of all the Bravo shows. She received a starred review from Publishers Weekly for *Talk Dirty to Me*, won a Romantic Times Reviewers' Choice Award for *Kiss and Hell*, along with many review site recommended reads and reviewer top pick awards.

Dakota lives in the gorgeous state of Oregon with her real life hero and her dogs, and she loves hearing from readers!

Connect with Dakota online:

Twitter: https://twitter.com/DakotaCassidy

Facebook: https://www.facebook.com/DakotaCassidyFanPage

Join Dakota Cassidy's Newsletter, The Tiara Diaries: http://mad.ly/signups/100255/join

eBooks by Dakota Cassidy

Visit Dakota's website at http://www.dakotacassidy.com for more information.

Accidentally Paranormal, a Paranormal Romantic Comedy series

Interview With an Accidental—a free introductory guide to the girls of the Accidentals!

1. The Accidental Werewolf

2. Accidentally Dead

3. The Accidental Human

4. Accidentally Demonic

5. Accidentally Catty

6. Accidentally Dead, Again

7. The Accidental Genie

8. The Accidental Werewolf 2: Something About Harry

9. The Accidental Dragon

10. Accidentally Aphrodite

11. Accidentally Ever After

12. Bearly Accidental

13. How Nina Got Her Fang Back

14. The Accidental Familiar

A Lemon Layne Mystery, a Contemporary Cozy Mystery Series

1. Prawn of the Dead

2. Play That Funky Music White Koi

3. Total Eclipse of the Carp

Witchless In Seattle Mysteries, a Paranormal Cozy Mystery series

1. Witch Slapped

2. Quit Your Witchin'

3. Dewitched

4. The Old Witcheroo

5. How the Witch Stole Christmas

Wolf Mates, *a Paranormal Romantic Comedy series*

1. An American Werewolf In Hoboken
2. What's New, Pussycat?
3. Gotta Have Faith
4. Moves Like Jagger
5. Bad Case of Loving You

A Paris, Texas Romance, *a Paranormal Romantic Comedy series*

1. Witched At Birth
2. What Not to Were
3. Witch Is the New Black
4. White Witchmas

Non-Series

1. Whose Bride Is She Anyway?
2. Polanski Brothers: Home of Eternal Rest
3. Sexy Lips 66

The Hell, *a Paranormal Romantic Comedy series*

1. Kiss and Hell
2. My Way to Hell

The Plum Orchard, *a Contemporary Romantic Comedy series*

1. Talk This Way
2. Talk Dirty to Me
3. Something to Talk About
4. Talking After Midnight

The Ex-Trophy Wives, *a Contemporary Romantic Comedy series*

1. You Dropped a Blonde On Me
2. Burning Down the Spouse
3. Waltz This Way

CPSIA information can be obtained
at www.ICGtesting.com
Printed in the USA
LVHW011914230719
625024LV00015B/1051/P

9 781544 729770